D0403282

TWELVE GREAT
BLACK CATS

TWELVE
GREAT

illustrated by VERA BOCK

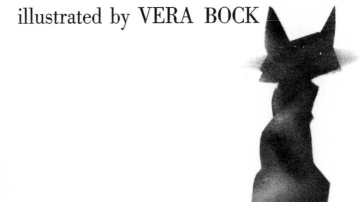

BLACK CATS

And Other Eerie Scottish Tales

by SORCHE NIC LEODHAS

E. P. DUTTON & CO., INC.
NEW YORK

Published simultaneously in Canada by Clarke,
Irwin & Company Limited, Toronto and Vancouver

SBN: 0-525-41575-0   LCC: 73-135855

Printed in the U.S.A.
First Edition

This book is for
Denise Dawn Digby
A's òige an fhine againne

S.N.L.

And to
Louis Robert Risser Hoffman
Móran taing

J.J.D.

To Kit,
One Great Cat

V.B.

Contents

Introduction

Ghost stories, tales of the supernatural, and of odd and inexplicable happenings are the gossip of the people, passed around as they sit by the fire of a stormy evening. Some are told at *ceilidhs*, where folk gather to tell stories, to sing beloved old songs, and, if someone has brought a fiddle, or in later days an accordion, to step out the intricate measures of Scottish strathspeys, Gay Gordons, jigs, and reels. There is always time for a story or two or three at a *ceilidh*, and many that are told are sure enough to send shivers down the hearers' spines. Fortunately, not all these Scottish tales are frightful. The Scots love to laugh, although that fact does not seem to be universally known, and they are not adverse to poking a sly bit of fun at themselves once in a while, as they do in the tale of "The Ghost of Hamish MacDonald."

It is impossible to put a date or an author to any supernatural story I have ever heard. Some of them one recognizes as fairly recent because their backgrounds mention modern things, but others, by their settings, show that they spring from days long gone. The important thing is that these tales, young or old, are still being told by word of mouth, and that their stock, unlike that of the folk tales, is still being added to. I have heard one particularly gruesome story of the haunting of a house in Aberdeen by the ghost of a child who died in 1945.

Not all the eerie stories of Scotland are ghost stories, however. There are tales of demons, fetches, monsters, and many other strange phenomena as well. In my own family we have a number of stories that are peculiarly our own. There were, for instance, two cousins of my grandmother who could communicate their thoughts to each other when they were apart. This happened to the good of the family one stormy autumn eve. Wullie had not done his lesson well and was kept at home to study it while his cousin Calum was sent to fetch in the cows. Wullie was sitting with his nose in his book, toasting his toes by the fire, when suddenly he lifted his head and sat up as if listening to something outside the house.

He said in a moment, "Calum is saying the broon coo is i' the boglach."

"Get back to your book," his mother bade him, not paying him much heed, thinking it a trick of Wullie's to get out with Calum. But Wullie tossed his book aside and shouted, "Rin and fetch my father and the men, for Wullie is saying he canna hauld her longer 'an she's going doon fast."

His mother, struck by his excitement, rushed out to

the byre and told her husband that Calum was saying the "broon coo" was stuck in the bog. He waited to ask no questions, but called the men, and they rushed off with ropes and ladders to the bog. Sure enough, there was the broon coo and she was being sucked into the bog, with Calum doing his best to keep her head above the mire. They got her out, but not without some difficulty, and if it had not been for Calum and Wullie they'd have lost her that day.

"Och, weel," said Wullie. "'Twas too far to run hame for help and I couldna leave the coo to herself wi' nane tae hauld her heid up, so I just tauld Wullie to send the men."

Well—that's one of the queer tales that have come down to me, and I have no doubt that every Scottish family could match it if they liked to. As for myself, I do believe that if you were to spread out the map of Scotland before me, I could tell you some strange and supernatural tale I've heard about almost every town and village that appears upon that map. In this book are ten of these stories, from ten Scottish towns lying between the Border and John o' the Groats, north, south, east, and west.

Sorche Nic Leodhas

TWELVE GREAT
BLACK CATS

Twelve Great Black Cats
and the Red One

FOLK will tell you that the days of signs and omens, witches, wizards, and warlocks, and the like are past, and only to be found in old wives' tales told to frighten silly bairns. But there's a man in Auchinogie who'll stand up against all the doubting folk who call such things superstitions, and with good reason. For did he not once have an uncommonly queer experience himself?

Murdo MacTaggart, his name was, and you'd look far before you'd find a more God-fearing, sober, and honest man. He had never been one to give up his mind to foolish fancies, so it surprised him a lot when things turned out the way they did. There he was, come day, go day, going about his affairs, taking his boat out at night with his nets and his fishing gear all in order, and coming in with his load of fish in the misty dawn. Each time was like the time before it, and nothing ever out of the way, until he met up with the great black cats.

It was upon an All Hallowmass Eve that it happened. The rest of the men told him he'd do better to stay at home and go to church, and not go out in his boat to fish that night, but Murdo only laughed and said, "The better the day, the better the deed!"

Down to the shore he went, but before he even got to his boat, all of a sudden a terrible storm blew up, with lightning flashing and thunder rolling, and the wind tearing by in a gale. There was a hut above the shore where the fishermen kept their nets and oars and fishing gear of one sort and another, and Murdo took shelter there while waiting for the storm to pass by.

While he waited he heard a queer sort of sound outside, and he looked out to see what made it. It was a very queer sight he saw, for there were twelve great black cats, and another, even bigger than the rest, with fur the color of a red fox, who seemed to be their leader, and they were all coming toward the hut. Murdo looked them over and did not care at all for what he saw. He drew back into the hut and sat down upon a stool in the corner there.

The red one led the twelve great black cats up to the door of the hut. They all crowded into the small space within and the black ones sat themselves down in a circle about the red one.

4.

Said the red one to the great black cats, "Why should we be sitting here in silence? Come now! Raise your voices in a coronach to Murdo MacTaggart."

And every cat opened its mouth and yowled out the coronach, and a good long and loud one it was, too, fit to nearly split the walls of the hut. What with the din of the storm without and the caterwauling of the creatures within, Murdo was not sure that he'd be able to come through it alive.

When the great black cats came to the end of the coronach, they sat still in their places, but the eyes of every one of them were fixed expectantly on Murdo.

The red one, giving a pleasant purr, said to Murdo, "Come along now, Murdo! You must pay for the grand coronach the cats have sung to you."

"Pay for it!" said Murdo. "What way would I be needing a coronach anyway, and me not being dead? What would I be paying them with, forbye?"

"That I cannot tell you," said the red one. "But singing whets the appetite. You had better pay them soon, man, for I can see the light of their hunger in their eyes."

Murdo looked at the glowing green eyes of the great black cats and shuddered. He looked to the left of him and he looked to the right of him, and saw nothing he could use to pay for the coronach, which he hadn't wanted anyway. Then he looked in front of him, over the heads of the great black cats and their leader, the red one, and in the field above the shore he saw an old wether and a bony old cow, standing with their backs against the storm.

5.

The beasts were not Murdo's. They belonged to the laird, but Murdo was beyond caring who owned what. He pointed to the old sheep and cried out, "Take the old wether over there on the lea for your pay."

Up the black cats sprang and hightailed it through the door, and up the shore onto the lea. They fell upon the wether and it did not last them long, for in no time there was naught left of the laird's wether but a neat heap of well-picked white bones.

Back they came in a trice before Murdo had time to figure out a way to escape from them. Down they sat again in a ring with the red one in the middle as before.

"Why be silent?" said the red one to the great black cats. "Sing a coronach to Murdo MacTaggart."

The cats began to yowl a coronach, and what with the crack of lightning and the roll of thunder and the rain pelting down on the roof and lashing the sides of the hut, the clamor, inside and out together, was terrible to hear.

They got to the end of the coronach at last and sat still, all glaring at Murdo with their green eyes opened wide.

"Come, Murdo," the red one said. "Pay them now for singing the coronach to you."

There were no two ways about it. Whether it was his or not, the laird's cow would have to go to the cats. Murdo pointed a finger to the creature and told them, "There's a cow up there on the lea. Take that for your pay."

The cow was old and had but little flesh upon her, so the cats finished her faster than they had the sheep.

Soon they were back at the hut again, and all that they left behind was a heap of shining bones on the lea beside those of the sheep.

Up to the hut they came again, and the red one bid them sing another coronach to Murdo MacTaggart. And once again the great black cats raised their voices and yowled out their song.

Murdo was in a desperate case, for the wether was gone and the cow was gone and he had naught to pay them for the coronach, which he hadn't asked for and had never wanted. He had it in his mind that this time it was his own bones the great black cats would be leaving behind in a neat little heap.

Then just as he was giving up hope and saying his prayers for what he thought was the last time, he looked over the heads of the cats and out the door. What did he see but the laird's big deerhound, a big rangy long-legged creature who could outrun the swiftest stag. The hound was sniffing about the piles of bones as if perplexed to find them there, and at that moment the coronach came to an end.

Murdo did not wait for the red one to bring up the subject. He lifted a finger and pointed it at the laird's dog, and cried out, "There's your pay!"

The cats flew out of the hut in a body, but the deerhound saw them coming. He gathered his legs beneath him and took off with a mighty bound that carried him halfway across the lea. After that first leap the deerhound put his mind on getting away quickly from the place. He moved with such speed that he made a tunnel through the torrents of the rain, and it was a good long time before the hole he made closed up after him again.

The great black cats flew over the lea and up the road after the deerhound, and the red one with them. As soon as Murdo found himself alone, he got himself out of the hut as fast as he could and ran into the wood that stood on the other side of the lea, hoping to make his escape undiscovered. He was going along the path as fast as his legs would carry him, making his way toward home, when he heard the cats coming back again, and in a great state of anger they were, because the deerhound had been too fleet and had got away. They began to search through the wood, looking for Murdo among the bushes and trees, and Murdo knew that there were too many of them for him to keep out of their way for long. One or the other of them would be sure to come across him soon.

There was a very tall tree beside him, with a trunk that was bare of branches almost three-fourths of the way up, and up the tree Murdo went, climbing it as a sailor climbs a mast. He settled himself on a good stout branch near the top and watched to see what went on below.

The big black cats were going about searching for him among the trees and bushes. Murdo grinned to himself to see them and thought himself safe up there, so high in the top. But his joy soon turned to dismay, for the red one came along and, looking up, spied him among the branches and called to his companions, "You can give up your search, for I've found Murdo

MacTaggart for you. There he is in the treetop, and we'll soon have him down."

"That you'll not!" said Murdo to himself.

But at that moment one of the great black cats began to climb the tree. When Murdo saw the creature coming, he drew his dirk from his belt and waited until the cat was almost up to his hiding place. The cat reached out with claws spread to grab him, but Murdo stabbed it to the heart with a quick thrust of his dirk. I' the cat ever had nine lives it must have lost the other eight before Murdo finished it off, for its body hurtled to the ground and there it lay dead.

A second cat then came climbing up the tree, and then a third one, and Murdo killed both of them.

"Hold!" said the red one to his companions who were left. "We'll not get him down that way! May ill luck befall him, he'll kill us all before we're through, if we continue to climb the tree."

He gathered the great black cats about him to talk the matter over, and at last the red one said, "If we cannot climb up and fetch him down, we'll bring the tree down with him in it, and catch him that way."

So the black cats gathered about the tree and began to dig the earth away from it with their claws, and when they came to a root they chewed through it with their sharp white teeth. When they cut through the first big root, the tree gave a shiver and listed to one side, and Murdo began to shake with fear. He opened his mouth and gave a great cry for help.

There was a church on the other side of the wood

9.

and the priest was just coming out with the people around him. He heard Murdo's shout and said to one of the men beside him, "That was the cry of one in great trouble. I may be needed. I must go."

"Wait now, Father," the man told him. " 'Tis a bad night for you to be going out. Let it be until we hear if the shout is raised again."

"Och, well, then," said the priest. "So let it be." But he went back into the church to fetch the things that might be needed, should the call come again.

At the tree the cats were digging with mad haste, and soon they had uncovered another root, and they bit it through. The tree began to lean heavily to the side, and Murdo gave a second wild shout for help.

"To be sure," said the priest. "That is a man whose need is great. Let us go quickly!"

The man beside him made no further objection, but with a nod here and a beckoning finger there he drew a dozen men from among the crowd at the church, and all of them went with the priest toward the wood.

The cats had uncovered the last big root and were chewing at it wildly. The root parted and the tree fell down with a crash just as the priest and the men with him came into sight. Murdo gave one last loud shout and climbed into the branches as high as he could, with the cats springing up to catch him and drag him down, and he with his dirk in hand to defend himself to his last breath. The men rushed forward to rescue Murdo, but the priest was before them. He was a wise old man, that priest, and he knew at once what he had to deal with. He had his holy water bottle in hand, and he opened it as he ran. He sprinkled the blessed water over the big black cats, making sure that every one of them had his full share.

"Begone, Satan, and you demons from hell! Begone!" he cried. "I bid you leave the soul and body of this man alone!"

The red one leaped high into the air and off he flew and soon was seen no more, but he left a great stench of smoke and brimstone behind him. As for the great black cats, they lay about on the ground beside the tree they had cut down. It was a strange thing about those great black cats, for when men went up to them to examine them where they lay, they were not cats at all but only great black cat skins lying upon the ground, with neither bones nor flesh within them!

So that was how Murdo MacTaggart was saved on that wild stormy night, not from a pack of great black cats with a red one for their leader, but from Auld Clootie, the de'il himself, with a pack of his demons he'd brought along with him from hell.

It taught Murdo a lesson, for never again did he go down to the shore to go fishing on an All Hallowmass Eve.

The Honest Ghost

WHEN the old Laird of Thistleton died it caused very little stir in the neighborhood. The demesne was large and there were many tenants on it: farmers, crofters, shepherds on the various steadings; a miller who tended a mill beside a busy stream; and numerous villagers, for the village of Balnacairn lay within the estate. But the Laird was an old man and had lived out his time. Although respected, he was not regretted much. No one was greatly concerned about his passing or troubled about the future. The old Laird was dead, God rest his soul, and now there would be a new laird to take over. It was expected things would be going on in the way they had always done before.

He died quite suddenly, but quietly, in his sleep on a cold and frosty October night, having just come home shortly before from a visit to the minister at Balnacairn village six miles away. For an old man he was unusually vigorous and had made the journey to the village and back that night on foot.

He was laid to rest in the churchyard, and those who had come to his funeral to pay their respects, if not to mourn, turned away and left him lying there among those of his family who for generations had been buried there.

Folk thereabout agreed that there was little to be said against the old Laird. To be sure, he was crabbed and cross-grained, and easily provoked into a rage. But as a master, he was just and fair-minded. And he was honest. Such a man, one could be certain, would rest peacefully in his grave.

Yet, soon after the old Laird's death, it became apparent that the old man's spirit had not found the rest and peace that were his due.

The first word of it came on a cold damp evening about six weeks or so after the old Laird's funeral. The folk of Balnacairn village, alarmed at hearing the sounds of horses' hoofs pounding and the rumble of the wheels of a heavy cart, coming down the road that led into the town, ran to their doors to find out what could be the matter.

Presently, two horses and the wagon they hauled loomed out of the misty drizzle and stopped before the inn. The villagers crowded about the wagon and found the driver, Lang Tammas the carter, lying against the wooden back of the seat, and shaking like a man in a palsy. He stared at them with wide open eyes, and his face was as white as bolted flour. It was a while before they could get any words out of him that made sense. Something had certainly given the man a terrible shock. They helped him down from the cart and took him into the inn, where the innkeeper brought him a wee glass of brandy to soothe his nerves, and after a while he began to come to himself again. But when he could talk what he said didn't have much sense in it at all.

Lang Tammas had gone over to the mill which stood a few miles beyond Thistleton Manor to take some sacks of corn to be ground for the minister of Balnacairn. It was when he was coming back that he got the terrible fright. As he came up to the gates of Thistleton Manor he saw a man standing in the middle of the drive between the stone gateposts. The mist was rising heavier there because of the burn that ran along beside the road, so he couldn't see the man distinctly at first, but he looked familiar to Lang Tammas. It wasn't until the carter drove right up close that he got a good look at the man. It was then that Tammas saw that it was the old Laird of Thistleton himself!

"The old Laird, it was, and he stepping out toward the cart, I'm telling you," said Tammas. "He had a big brass lantern in his hand. It was not lit, and he held it up and shook it at me. Then he called me by name, he did. 'Look ye here, Lang Tammas!' said he, and made to come closer, but I was in no mind to wait to hear what he would say. I whipped up the horses and

15.

hastened away at a gallop, and left him by the gate there!"

Well, that was the tale Lang Tammas told, and there were some who believed him but there were more who did not, and the latter said that Lang Tammas had a wee bit too much to drink with the miller, while waiting for the minister's corn to be ground.

No doubt the matter would have been forgotten after a while if nothing else had happened, but a month later the old Laird appeared again, and not in the dusk of a misty evening but in the clear light of day.

It was Jamie the Post who got sight of the Laird this time, while Jamie was bringing the post bags from the railway station at Balquidder to the post mistress at Balnacairn. Jamie was ambling along in the post cart at an easy pace, it not being his way to hurry himself at any time. When he was passing the gates of Thistleton Manor he gave a careless glance up the drive and there in the doorway of the gatehouse, just inside the manor gates, he saw the old Laird of Thistleton standing, with the big brass lantern in his hand. The Laird waved the lantern at Jamie, but Jamie did not wait to see if the Laird would come nearer, or to hear if he called Jamie by name. Jamie whipped up the pony that drew the post cart, and they dashed madly down the road and into the village of Balnacairn, and folk there said his speed was an achievement that Jamie never equalled before or after.

No one could blame what Jamie saw on his having had a drink or two too many, for it was well known that Jamie was a strong temperance man and had never in his life taken a drink. Maybe there was something in it after all, folk told each other. Nobody cared to talk much about it, now that the Laird had been seen twice. Such things don't bear talking about that happen so close to home. But nobody, if he could help it, went anywhere near Thistleton Manor after the day the old Laird was seen for the second time.

Well, the old Laird's estate was settled at last, and as he had neither wife nor bairns of his own, he left all he had to his nephew, the only son of a brother who had gone to Australia and settled there. The title went to the nephew, too, so now there was a new Laird of Thistleton, as well as the old Laird, who seemed to be still lingering about the place.

Folk began to wonder how the old Laird would get along when the new Laird came to take over the estate.

The new Laird did not come home to Thistleton Manor at once. He had established a business where he lived and needed time to dispose of it profitably. Besides, the sea journey was long and the time of year was not the best for traveling. The new Laird and his wife had a very young bairn and thought they'd rather wait until the child was older and the conditions of weather better before making so long a journey with him. So the estate was put into the hands of an estate agent in Edinburgh, who was to see to the managing of the lands and the farms and the tenants, until the new Laird came home. As for the manor house itself, the agent was to find a tenant for it, with a short lease of no more than a year, if he could.

The agent had no trouble in finding a tenant. It was

a desirable property, as the notice in the papers said, and the house was nicely furnished and well kept up. The agent found not only one tenant, but three. One after another they came—and left—all driven out, one after another, because they could not bear the sight of the old Laird with the big brass lantern in his hand.

After the third tenant left, in a high state of indignation, there were no more tenants, because by that time the word had gone around that the place was haunted, and as the estate agent said, "Who in the world would ever want to rent a haunted house?"

That was the way matters stood when the new Laird of Thistleton finally came over the seas to take up his estates. He did not go immediately to Thistleton Manor, but stopped in Edinburgh to talk to the agent whom he had put in charge of his affairs.

He settled his wife and bairn at a comfortable hotel and went to the office of the agent. He had never been in Scotland before and knew very little about his inheritance. He found the agent in his office, and the minute he laid eyes on the man the new Laird knew that something was amiss. He knew, too, that the agent did not want to tell him what it was. The new Laird could not lay his finger on the trouble. The agent seemed ready enough to talk about the estate. He brought out a map with the demesne marked upon it: the mill, the farms, the church, the village, the manor and all in their places, with the names of the tenants beside them. He brought out the accounts and they were all in order. No trouble about anything there, as the new Laird could see for himself. Yet the agent seemed to be uneasy about something. What on earth could it be?

The new Laird picked up the accounts and looked at them again, and something caught his eye that he had not noticed before.

"I'm a plain man, and I'll ask you a plain question," he told the agent. "What is wrong with the manor house?"

"Nothing at all!" the agent answered quickly. Too quickly, the new Laird said to himself.

"The house is in fine shape. Well-cared for, and nicely furnished. You could not ask for a better-kept house."

"If that is so," the new Laird said. "Why is it that in the first six months after my uncle's death three tenants, one after another, signed up for the house, expecting to stay for a year, and every one of them cleared out before the end of a month? And since the last one left, no one has taken the manor house at all? What is wrong with the place?"

"Well," said the agent reluctantly. "They say it's haunted!"

The new Laird of Thistleton looked at the agent in disbelief. "Haunted!" he exclaimed. "It could not be. My father loved the place and never tired of talking of it. He'd have taken delight in an old family ghost, and I'm sure we'd have heard about it if there had been one there."

"It is not an old family ghost that was seen," the agent said. "At any rate, not a *very* old ghost. In fact, it is the ghost of your late uncle, as I understand. They say he carries a great brass lantern and shakes it in their faces. Most alarming, I am sure."

The new Laird looked at the agent in silence for a while. Then he got up to take his leave. "I'll look into it," he promised, and went his way.

The new Laird of Thistleton went back to his hotel and told his wife what the agent had said.

"My goodness!" said she. "Poor Uncle Andrew! He must find it very uncomfortable to be a ghost. I wonder what makes him do it?"

"So do I," said the new Laird. "And what's more, I mean to find out."

They decided to go, not to Thistleton Manor, but to the village of Balnacairn. The village was only six miles from the manor, which was no distance at all, and the agent had said there was a very good inn where they would be able to stay. They felt that the inn would be the best place to carry on their investigations from, and besides, the new Laird's wife was not sure it would be a good thing for the baby if they went to stay at Thistleton Manor and Uncle Andrew were to appear and shake his big brass lantern at him.

Fortunately, they were able to find lodging at the inn, and the landlady was pleased when she learned that it was the new Laird and his family who were sheltering under her roof. Perhaps it was the pleasure that the honor thus paid gave her that loosened her tongue. At any rate, before a day had passed, she had told the new Laird and his wife all about the way the old Laird's ghost had appeared to Lang Tammas the carter and to Jamie the Post, and as the tenants had fled to the inn from Thistleton Manor, she could tell about their experiences too.

The new Laird and his wife were pleasant folk and friendly, and not the sort to set themselves up above others, as folk said, so the tenantry accepted them at once. It wasn't that they had anything against the old Laird, you understand, but they could see that this new man would make a very good laird. So nobody minded at all answering any questions the new Laird and his lady asked.

What the new Laird and his wife wanted to find out was, what kept the old Laird from resting quietly in his grave? What sort of man had he been when he was alive?

Well, folk said, he was a crabbed old creature, so he was, but he was just.

He worked his men hard, but then he was a hard worker himself. And he was honest. He always gave an honest day's pay for an honest day's work. He had a terrible temper and would fly into a sudden rage if anyone crossed him, but to tell the truth, he never was angry without a good reason. He couldn't abide dishonesty, being an honest man himself. He could stretch a penny farther than any other man, but a man could count on getting what was due him, although probably he'd get no more. He was an honest man, the old Laird was.

The minister, who had been the old man's only close friend, smiled when he was asked what the old Laird was like. "Not so bad as he liked to make out," he said. "He was a bit crusty and short-tempered at times, but he was more honest than any other man I know. It would have been as impossible for the Laird to lie, or cheat, or steal, as for him to pick up Ben Nevis and hold it in one hand."

Everybody did feel sorry for the new Laird and his lady, with them coming such a long distance only to find that the manor house was not habitable on account of the ghost. They would have helped gladly, but though they racked their brains, they could not say what was troubling the old Laird so that he could not rest in his grave.

The new Laird and his wife put their heads together and compared notes on everything they had been told.

"The old Laird was a terrible old curmudgeon," said the new Laird.

"But he was honest," said his wife.

"He was a penny pincher," said the new Laird.

"But he was honest," said his wife.

"He had a way at times of flying into a terrible rage," said the new Laird.

"But he was honest," said the Laird's wife. "No matter what anyone said about him, every single one of them said that he was honest. I don't think that a man as honest as your Uncle Andrew would be haunting Thistleton Manor just to keep you away. Not after he'd left it to you in his will!"

"I think you are right," her husband said. "There's no doubt about his honesty. Everybody speaks of it."

His wife said nothing for a while, then she said slowly, "There is something else about your uncle that everybody mentions. When they speak about his ghost,

22.

I mean. The tenants told the agent, Lang Tammas the carter and Jamie the Post told the folk here at Balnacairn. When anyone ever says anything about the ghost they say and he shook his big brass lantern in his face!' *Everyone* says it."

They looked at each other for a minute in silence. Then, "Tomorrow," said the new Laird, "we will go to Thistleton Manor."

"And see if there is a big brass lantern there," said his wife.

So the next day they left the baby with the landlady at the inn and borrowed a pony and cart from the landlord, and off they went.

They went up the drive and got out of the cart, and the young Laird opened the door with the key the agent had given him. They went into the house and searched from room to room, upstairs and down. Not a sign of a big brass lantern did they see—nor of the old Laird's ghost, for that matter.

"Uncle Andrew's lantern must be the ghost of a lantern," the new Laird said, as they came down to the hall again.

His wife had gone to the other end of the passage and was standing before a door. "What door is this?" she asked, trying the knob. "It's locked. Where does it lead to?"

"Probably into the garden," said the new Laird.

"I don't think it does," said his wife. "The rooms on either side go back farther. I think it's a room—a small one."

"Of course it is!" the new Laird said. "I know what

it is. It's my uncle's estate office. The agent told me about it. He locked it up when he took charge of the estate, because there were private papers here and he wanted them to be kept safe. Wait a minute! I think he gave me the key."

The key was found and the door was opened. The first thing they saw was the big brass lantern, standing alone on the shelf above the old Laird's desk.

The new Laird's wife took down the lantern. "Look," she said. There was a tag tied by a string to the ring at the top. They saw that there were words written carefully on the tag. "The minister's lantern. Balnacairn," they read. They looked at each other.

"Poor Uncle Andrew!" the new Laird's wife said. "All he wanted was for someone to take the lantern back to its rightful owner. It didn't belong to him, and he couldn't rest in his grave knowing it hadn't been returned."

They took the lantern back to the minister that very day. He took it in his hands. "Why, I'd forgotten he had it," the minister said. "I remember now. He borrowed it the last time he was here, before he died. He had stayed late, for we got to talking and never noticed the time, and it was dark when he started out for home. So I let him take the lantern to light him home."

The next day the Laird and his wife and his bairn packed up and moved into Thistleton Manor. They were quite sure the old Laird's ghost was at rest, now that the lantern was back where it belonged. And they were right.

Folk kept a close watch for a while, but everything

24.

at the manor seemed to be going on very well, and as far as anybody could tell the ghost was gone for good. So Lang Tammas the carter began to haul his corn to the mill, and Jamie the Post to carry the post bags along the road past Thistleton Manor again, instead of taking the longer road the way they'd been going since they met the old Laird's ghost.

The new Laird and his wife called their second son Andrew after the old Laird, and he was very like him in temperament, for he was given to spells of being crabbed and crusty, often flying into a rage. But his mother said she did not mind, as long as he grew up to be as honest as the old Laird, because the old Laird, as everyone always said, was a very honest man.

The Ghost of Hamish MacDonald,
The Fool of the Family

There once was a time when the MacLeods and the MacDonalds got into an argument about something or other, and what it was nobody remembers to this day. It was on a lonely moor over the hills it started, some distance from the homes of either party, and the lot of them should have had more sense than to make trouble there, since they were on territory belonging to some other clan. Well, the argument became a quarrel, and the quarrel led to a fight, and before anybody knew what was happening, the two clans were lined up on the moor facing each other, ready to do battle, with every man panting with eagerness to prove his side was in the right.

The opposing clans were pretty well matched. There were one hundred and twenty MacLeods and one hundred and twenty-one MacDonalds, but the extra MacDonald did not matter at all, because although he was a very hale and hearty lad and able to fight well enough if he put his mind to it, he was the fool of the family and bound to do everything amiss.

Now it was the custom of the MacDonalds, when they made ready for battle, that each man of the clan would find himself a big stone and carry it in his hand to a place that was judged to be well out of the line of battle, which place was decided upon beforehand. There each warrior laid down his stone to make a cairn. After the fighting was over, each man who survived the battle went, then, to the cairn and took up his stone again. By counting the stones that remained upon the ground they could find out the number of their companions who had perished in the fray that day.

One by one, the MacDonalds laid down their stones, and Hamish, the fool of the family, laid his on the cairn with the rest. Then they all cast their kilts and their plaids aside, and taking their swords in their hands, they hurled themselves, barelegged and barearmed, against the MacLeods with a great shouting of the MacDonald slogan, *"Dh'aindeòin co theireadh e"* (Gainsay me who dare).

Wherever the battle was thickest, there was Hamish, the fool of the family, wielding his sword with a will, but as he had a very bad habit of screwing his eyes tight shut every time he dealt a blow, he hit friend as often as foe, so that any warrior was unlucky who came within reach of his flailing sword.

As for himself, he had the good fortune of all fools, since those men amongst whom he fought were so intent on getting around him to fight with each other, that they seldom bothered to aim a blow at him.

Hamish might have gone on in this fashion, doing much to impede the efforts of both his own clansmen and their foes, if the pressure of the battle had not carried him close to the brink of a crag at the side of the moor. Fortune then favored the warriors in whose way Hamish had so manfully put himself, for, in some manner or other, he managed to trip over the blade of his own sword. With his face to the fighting men before him and his back to the top of the crag, he did not know his danger. He took a backward step and his feet found nothing to stand upon. Over the cliff he went, heels over head, and tumbled into the wee burn that ran below. He landed upon his head with a thump that might well have killed him entirely, had it not been for the special protection that Heaven gives to fools. As it was, his senses were knocked out of him, and he lay in a swoon, half in and half out of the burn, while the battle went on without him on the moor above.

His absence was not noticed by either the MacLeods or the MacDonalds, except for a feeling of relief that he was no longer in their way. Nobody saw him fall, nobody seemed to miss him at all, and the two clans went on fighting until the night began to fall.

With the gloaming the dewmists began to rise, and

29 .

the warriors saw that there was little likelihood of either side winning that day. All the fighting had brought neither one clan nor the other to the point of victory. The chiefs then held a consultation under a flag of truce, and decided to call it a draw, and to consider as settled the original cause of the dispute, which most of the lads had already forgotten in the joy of fighting for it anyway.

Then the MacLeods went off one way and the Mac-Donalds went off the other. Although much blood had been spilt, none of the wounds seemed likely to prove fatal, and all of the clansmen were able to withdraw from the battlefield in good order, each on his own two feet. All, that is, except Hamish MacDonald, the fool of the family, who still lay at the foot of the crag in the wee burn.

The MacDonalds marched up to the cairn of stones, and there each man of them took up a stone in his hand. When each man had done so, there was but one stone left upon the ground.

"That would be the marker for Hamish, the fool of the family," said the chief, and sent men to search about the moor to find the poor lad's body there. They hunted through the heather but not a sign of Hamish did they find, and at last the chief, who wanted to be well on his way before the night was darker, called them back again.

Everybody was puzzled that Hamish's body had not been found, but no one thought to look over the edge of the crag. What with the mist and the shadows of the gloaming, they'd not have been likely to see him anyway, down there.

"Leave it be," said the chief. "The stone shall bide where it is. Happen he's still alive, and if it be so, he'll get it when he comes along, and if he's dead it will show that we've lost one man in the fight."

So the MacDonalds gathered up their plaids and their kilts and put them on, and off they started on their journey home, leaving the one stone behind them lying alone on the ground.

They had not gone more than half a mile or so when they met the MacDonald piper who had come out to find them. He had not been in the battle with them that day, being himself away from home when the clan went off that morn. When they told him that all the warriors had come through the battle safely except for Hamish, who was missing, but whether dead or alive they could not say, the piper shook his head with concern.

"Lest he be dead," said the piper, "he must have the coronach played for him. And should he happen to be alive, 'twill do him no harm, forbye."

So the piper blew up his bagpipes and led the clan homeward, playing the coronach to Hamish MacDonald as he went.

It was just at this moment that Hamish came to his senses and found himself in the waters of the burn. 'Twas lucky for him they were no deeper or he'd have drowned long since. The evening breezes played about him, cold and chill, as he got to his feet, unsteady and shivering, with naught to cover him but his long white shirt, and it dripping burn water from neck to hem.

He clambered up to the top of the crag and peered about him in the twilight shadows. De'il a MacLeod or a MacDonald was in sight upon the moor. Hamish limped over to the place where the clan had made its cairn and saw the one stone that remained upon the ground.

"One stone!" exclaimed Hamish. "Och, then! One of our brave laddies gave up his life in the fight this day. Poor body! I wonder now, who would it be?"

So he sat down beside the stone to think it over. It was then that from the distance the mournful sound of the music of the piper came floating across the moor to his ear. A horrid thought came into his mind.

"Losh!" he cried. "There go the MacDonald men home, taking their wee stones awa' wi' them! Seeing that there is but one stone left behind and me the only man here, the stone must be my own. Och, dule and woe! Then it's myself that's dead, and that mournful piping I hear is the coronach the MacDonald piper is playing for me!"

Not for a minute did Hamish doubt that he was dead, although he could not understand how it had come about. He had a few good slashing cuts upon his body but none so bad that they could cause a man to die. The last thing he remembered was getting his legs tangled up with his sword, so that he stumbled over the crag. It was the fall over the crag that killed him, he decided at last.

"Och, weel," he thought, "folk told me my head was

awful saft. Many's the time the laird said to me, 'Hamish, have a care, now. Ye're richt saft in the head, my lad!' I ken well, now, that it was naught but the truth he was telling me, and the saftness of my head has brought about my death, for upon my head I fell."

So Hamish sighed dolefully, and sat down upon the ground beside his wee stone, to think about his sad fate.

The night grew darker, and a hound bayed in the distance, and a midnight cock crowed at a croft far over the moor, but Hamish sat on thinking, as the hours of the night went by. He had never been a ghost before, but he did not feel much different than he had before he died. He wondered if it was in the natural way of things for a ghost to feel so terribly cold and wet. But that did not trouble him so much as the question of what he was going to do next.

The stars began to flicker out in the sky and the morning breeze came riding by to welcome in the dawn. An early curlew raised its harsh note, flying high in the lift above, on its way back to the sea.

Hamish came to a decision at last, as the sounds of waking life around him roused him from his thoughts. Ghost or not, his place was with his own folk, not upon this far off and unfamiliar moor. He would rise up and make his way home, to bide with his own folk again.

He rose to his feet to start upon the homeward journey, and suddenly a fresh difficulty presented itself to his mind. He had no notion of which way to turn, whether to the right or to the left. "Och, I'm lost, to be sure!" Hamish cried.

There was a track running through the heather across

the moor, and while Hamish stood trying to make his mind up which way to go he heard the sound of someone coming along the track. It was neither dark nor daylight, but that time of early morn when the world is just making ready to show a bit of itself but is still wrapped in the mists of night.

Through the fog that hung over the heather Hamish saw a farm lad walking slowly behind two cows that he was driving along the track.

"I'll ask the lad to gi'e me the directions," said Hamish to himself, stepping out to meet the lad. The lad was idling along, switching the dew from the heather with a stick he carried in his hand. As he was not looking up he did not see Hamish at first.

Now Hamish had lain long in the burn, and then had sat thinking all through the chill night in his wet shirt, and it had given him a terrible frog in his throat so that his voice came out in a hoarse deep croak. As the lad came near, Hamish spoke up and said, "I am the ghost of Hamish MacDonald. Will ye gi'e me—?" He had no chance to say more, for the lad jumped a foot in the air and dropped his stick, and when he looked up again and saw Hamish standing before him in his wet shirt, with the morning mist swirling about him, the poor body let out a terrible screech.

"Och, a ghost!" he cried. "Aye, I'll gi'e ye the kyne. Take them!" And turning about he ran off the way he had come like the wind itself.

Hamish stood and looked after the lad and wondered what made him run away. He meant him no harm. Well, the lad had told him to take the cows, and a man would be daft to turn down an offer of that sort, so Hamish took the cows. He picked up the stick the lad had flung away and started to drive the cows along the track, going the other way from that in which the lad had run away.

Hamish had not gone far on his way, when again he heard someone coming along the track. Hamish stopped and waited for the newcomer to appear, for he still wanted to know the way to go home. Soon an old body appeared, stepping along the misty track, leading a shaggy wee pony with creels full of farm stuff fastened on either side.

Hamish went up beside her and croaked out, "I am the ghost of Hamish MacDonald!"

But the old wife let him say no more. "Ochone!" she shrieked. "Then it was the truth the laddie said, and me not believing him, may the Lord forgive me!" Away she went over the moor, and as she ran she cried back over her shoulder, "Take the wee pony, 'tis yours if you're wanting it, but leave me be!" And soon she was out of sight.

Hamish could not understand such carryings-on. Why should folk mind a ghost who bore them no ill will and did not threaten them at all? But she had said for him to take the pony, and such a gift he could not despise. So he took the pony's bridle in his hand, and driving the two cows before him, he went on his way.

The track led through a bit of wood, and though dawn was close to breaking, it was very still and dark there underneath the leafy branches of the trees. As Hamish, with his cows and his pony, moved along

through the wood, he heard the sound of wheels coming briskly toward him. Hamish hoped that this time
he'd have better luck in learning which way would lead
him home. So he waited by the side of the track. Soon
a cart came rolling along through the misty shadows of
the wood. The cart was drawn by a wee tidy donkey,
and in the front of the cart, driving the beastie along,
was a jolly fat farmer, whistling a merry lilt as he came.

Hamish left his cows and the pony by the roadside.
He stepped into the middle of the road, and held up
his hand for the farmer to stop. The farmer left off his
whistling when he laid eyes on Hamish in his wet white
shirt, and with the signs of battle upon him. It was
plain to be seen that the farmer did not like the sight.
But when Hamish croaked, "I am the ghost of Hamish
MacDonald. Will ye gi'e me—?" the farmer bided no
longer than the lad and the auld wife had done.

"A ghaist!" he cried in terror, leaping out of the cart
in a great hurry. "Aye—I'll give you whate'er you're
wanting, so long as you do not fash yourself with me!"
And out of the wood and over the moor he rushed away
from Hamish, and never stopped to look behind.

Hamish stood watching the farmer who was wasting
no time in his flight.

"The folk here about are unco queer," Hamish said to
himself. "I ne'er saw their like before. Lawks! They're
daft, the lot of them!"

Then, remembering that the farmer had said he
might have whatever he was wanting, he went over to
the cart. The cart was small but sturdy, and the sleek

little donkey looked to be a good creature. In the bed of the cart were several slatted crates in which there were a goose and a gander, a duck and a drake, and a half dozen plump hens, all of them making such a honking and quacking and clucking that a body could not hear himself think. They looked to be very fine fowl, so Hamish, since the farmer had told him to take whatever he wanted, took the lot—donkey, cart, geese, ducks, and hens. He tied the bridle of the wee shaggy pony to the back of the cart and tethered a cow at either side of the pony, then, getting into the cart, he drove on up the track away from the moor.

When he came out of the wood it was daybreak and folk were beginning to stir about, but they paid no heed to Hamish, all of them being busy at their morning's work. As for Hamish, he had taken a fair scunner against the folk in these parts, thinking them all daft feckless bodies, so he paid them no more heed than they did him.

So on and on he traveled, taking roads at random, following his nose where it led him, and trusting to luck to take him the right way. His trust was not misplaced, for late in the day, Hamish MacDonald came safely home.

As he drove down the glen to his own village, whom should he meet but the chief of the clan. The sight of Hamish with all his booty so dumbfounded the chief that he could not speak a word. He stood staring at Hamish with his mouth agape. Hamish sighed. He wondered if he was going to have the same trouble with the chief that he had had with the folk on the moor that morn. He clambered down from the cart and stepped up to the chief.

"I am the ghost of Hamish MacDonald," said he. The chief's mouth snapped shut, but he opened it again at once to give a great roar.

"That you're not!" shouted the chief.

"I'm not?" asked Hamish, feeling terribly bewildered.

"Nay, ye great coof! You're Hamish MacDonald himself, and every bit alive as myself! And will you tell me what you think you're doing, running about the countryside clad only in your shirt? Where's your plaid and your kilt, man?"

"Losh!" cried Hamish. "I forgot them entirely. I left them lying back there upon the moor."

"Where the de'il have you been, man?" demanded the chief. "All the night and all the day? And where did you get the cart and the creatures? You'll not be telling me you left the battle to go reiving! The Mac-Donalds have aye been warriors, I'll have you know. There's ne'er been a reiver in the clan since it began."

"I was not reiving," said Hamish, very much hurt by the accusation. "Och, I had a great fall o'er the crag back there where we was fighting, and when I started for home in the morning, I kept meeting the daftest class o' folk, and they all gave these things to me."

When the chief had got the whole story from Hamish, he gathered the men of the clan together to decide what should be done. There were some who said that Hamish should be made to take the cart and the beasties back where they belonged. But most of them said that move would be bound to stir up trouble. If the folk Hamish met believed that they had seen a ghost on the moor, it might be wise to let them go on thinking that way, for in that case they'd not be expecting to see their things again. As for Hamish's kilt and plaid, it would not be worthwhile for anyone to take the time to go so far to fetch them home. It was time Hamish had new ones anyway.

The chief looked about and found a wee croft for Hamish. He told Hamish to take his creatures there and settle himself down, and Hamish, being a good-natured biddable lad, did as he was told. With his cows, his geese, his ducks, and his hens, his wee shaggy pony, and his donkey and cart, he was as happy as any man might ever hope to be.

To tell the truth he was so much better at farming than at fighting that the chief persuaded him to give up fighting for good. He hung his sword up on the chimney breast and turned out to be a good crofter in the end.

After that, whenever the men of the MacDonald clan went out to battle, they had to get along without Hamish, the fool of the family.

The Weeping Lass at the
Dancing Place

OUTSIDE many a Scottish village, where the cross-roads meet, there will be a level bit of ground lying in one of the triangles made by the intersection of the roads. In the old days folk would be calling such a spot the dancing place, because it was the custom of the young lads and lasses of the neighborhood to gather there, to dance away the hours of a moonlit night. Generations of lively young feet trod down and packed the soil in these places, until the surface was as hard and smooth as stone. No fine laird and his lady could ever have found a grander floor to dance upon than a dancing place.

It was once in the summer twilight, a long, long time

ago, that a company of young folk gathered at such a dancing place to foot it gaily, by the light of the moon.

They came from all directions; those from the village on foot, and those who lived farther away on crofts or farmsteads, riding upon their shaggy wee Highland ponies or upon their workaday mares. Some of the lads came riding with their lasses perched on their saddles behind them, and some of them came walking with their sweethearts on their arms. Their gay voices rose sweetly on the fresh breeze of the summer evening, and the sound of talk and laughter filled the air as the young folk met.

Those who came alone soon found partners, except for one lass who came stealing along from the village, at the end of the merry line. She did not join the others but sat herself down in the shadows cast by a hedge along the road.

The voices of the dancers provided the music for their dancing. Having neither pipe nor fiddle to mark the measures, they moved to the tunes of the songs they sang, and if the breath of some of them failed in the exertion of the dance, there were always enough of the singers to keep the song going until the laggards could take up the tune again.

The lass who sat under the hedge made no move to join in the fun. Word had been brought to her in the early springtime, some months before, that her lover had been drowned in the sea during the herring fishing, and she had made a vow never to sing or dance again all her whole life long.

From the day they told her of her true love's death

she had spent all her time lamenting and weeping. Even in her sleep she dreamed of her loss, and the tears ran down her cheeks while she slept.

It was the grief of her life that she could not sit and mourn beside the grave of her dead lover, but the seaside village to which he had gone for the fishing was at a distance from his own home. When his body was washed ashore, the villagers had carried it to their own graveyard and buried it there.

Now the lass sat by herself in the shadow of the hedge, near the dancing place where she and her love had once been happy together, and watched and listened and wept.

While the dancers were merrymaking a man came cantering along the road on a great black horse. He pulled up his steed at sight of the merry throng, and swinging himself from its back, he hurried to join their sport. The dancers, intent upon their own amusement, paid him little heed, but opened their ranks to let him in. He, for his part, threw himself into the dance with a will. No voice laughed louder or sang more gaily, no foot moved more fleetly than that of the stranger in their midst.

So the night wore on, and many a reel and strathspey and jig was footed by the young folk, and many a gay lilt was sung. But all good things must come to an end. As the hour grew late, the dancers, tiring, began to steal away for home. One or two at a time they went at first, then in larger numbers, until the last stragglers in a body hurried away. No one was left then at the dancing place but the stranger who had ridden there upon his black horse and the lass who sat weeping under the hedge.

He strode up to the lass and stood looking down upon her.

"You were once a bonnie, bonnie lass," said he. "And you'd be bonnie again if your face were not so raddled with weeping and your eyes not so swollen red."

She buried her face in her hands and wept harder. "Why would I not be weeping?" said she. "The tears I'm shedding are for my true love who is dead."

"Greeting and grieving will not bring the dead back to life again," the stranger said roughly. "So much mourning serves no purpose but to make it so the dead cannot rest easy in their graves. Come, lass, dry your tears and hush your lament, and tread a measure with me!"

She looked up at him but could not see his face because of the tears in her eyes. She shook her head. "I will not dance," said she.

But he reached down and took her wrist in his hand, and pulling her to her feet, he drew her toward the dancing place. She held back and struggled with all her might, but he was stronger than she and he would not let her go. Against her will she found her feet were moving in the figures of the dance, while he whistled softly to mark the time of their steps.

"I will not!" she protested and tried to free herself.

"Aye, but you will!" said he, and she could not stop, because he whirled her so madly and held her so fast.

Then, she looked up at the face that bent above her. A shaft of the cold moonlight lay white upon it, and she cried out. The face she saw was that of the lover whom she had mourned so long! Her heart leaped for joy and she called him by name. "They told me you were dead!" she cried.

"Is that what they told you?" he asked.

"They said you were dead and long buried," said she.

"Did they say so?" he asked, and whirled her faster and faster in the dance.

"You will never leave me again?" she begged him.

"I must be on my way from here, lass," he told her. "Long before the break of dawn."

"Then I shall go too," the lass cried out. "Take me with you wherever you go!"

"My dwelling place is small and low," he told her. "I doubt you'd like it o'ermuch. The walls are damp and it is dark, and there is little more than room enough for me."

"With me to help we'll soon earn a better," the lass insisted stoutly. "I'll help with my hands and share your toil each day."

"You'd do better to find yourself a new love," he said.

"You shall not go without me," said she.

"Come then, if you must!" he said.

Then he took her up behind him on his great black horse, and off they galloped up the road the way he had come.

"Hold fast!" he bade her. "The time is short. We have a long way to go and I must be home before the break of day."

The black horse spurned the stones of the road with his hoofs until sparks flew out at either side. The wind came tearing after them, but never caught up with them as they sped by.

"Hold fast!" the lass's lover called to her over his shoulder, and at his command, she caught his belt in both her hands and held it tight.

Then a chill came over her. She felt so cold that she thought she could not bear it. She wondered that a summer night should freeze one to the bone like one of winter, but laid it to the speed at which they rode.

Her lover's garments whipped back against her. She wondered, as they touched her, why they felt so damp when no rain had fallen all along the way.

"Why is your cloak so wet?" she asked, but he made no reply at all.

The black horse raced faster and faster, through clachan and village, and over hill and down.

"Will we not soon be there?" the lass cried out in despair.

But her lover whipped his steed on through the night without an answering word.

Then, of a sudden, her shawl flew up into her face. She had to take one hand from his belt to pull the shawl down and wrap it about herself. When she reached to take hold of the belt again she grasped, instead, a handful of his linen shirt. The cloth was icy cold and heavy with moisture. "Why are your clothes so dripping wet!" she exclaimed. "Och, a body'd think you'd been riding through a storm, but no rain at all has fallen. See then, my own clothes are dry."

Just at that moment they came to the gate of a kirkyard where the kirk stood tall and dark with its graves on either side.

Her lover slowed his black horse down, and turned it in at the gate, bringing it to a stop among the graves at one side of the kirk.

"This is my dwelling place," he told her, as he alighted from his horse. "You gave me no rest in my grave. The sound of your voice lamenting kept me awake night and day. And if my clothes are wet, 'tis little wonder, for the tears you have shed have gathered and run down into the place where I lay. Now you shall cease your weeping and lie beside me in my grave, and I shall have peace at last."

The lass looked down at the face that was turned up to her own. She saw, with horror, that it was not a face at all, but a bony skull, and under the clothes that clung so wetly there was no warm living flesh, but only whitened bones. Then she knew that her lover was dead indeed, and it was his ghost that had brought her here.

"Come!" he said, and reached up to pull her down from the back of the horse.

But she cried, "Nay!" and slipped to the ground on the other side. She gathered up her skirts and ran away from him, faster than she'd ever run in all her life before.

He came after her, his bony hands outstretched to catch her. She felt his fingers take hold of the border of her shawl. But she cast off the shawl and ran on. She ran out from among the graves and down the path in front of the kirk, and through the gate of the kirkyard into the road. She was growing too short of breath to keep on running. She glanced over her shoulder to see how close he followed at her feet. But just at the moment she looked, the dawn broke in the eastern sky, and on every side the cocks began to crow to greet the morn.

Like a puff of mist dissolving, ghost and horse disappeared, and the lass saw naught behind her but the kirk and the kirkyard with its graves, peaceful in the first gray morning light.

The shock of relief at finding her pursuer gone was too great for the lass to bear. She lost her senses and fell to the road, and there she lay.

A milkmaid on her way to milk her cows found the lass lying there in the middle of the road, and ran to the village close by to fetch help. Men came and carried her to a house where kind hands took her in and cared for her, until she came to herself again.

They were curious to know what had happened to her, and when she told her story they were amazed. They might have thought that she had dreamed it all, or even that she was daft, if it had not been for the shawl.

She had told them of casting her shawl away, when the specter grasped it in his hand. And it was true she wore no shawl when she was found. It was two or three days later that one of the villagers went to the kirkyard to tidy the graves, and saw upon one of them what looked to be a bit of tartan cloth with fringe at the edge. He went to pick it up, wondering how it had come to lie there, but found that it was buried deep in the mound of the grave. Pull as he might, he could not get it out. Then he remembered the strange lassie's shawl, and hurried to tell his neighbors what he had found. They all ran to the kirkyard, and brought the lass with them.

" 'Tis my shawl," she told them. "I've had it many a year. I would not like to lose it."

But it was so firmly fixed in the soil that the strongest man in the village could not pull the shawl out. In the end they had to fetch shovels and dig it out. They dug all the way down to the coffin but still they could not pull the shawl away. It was not until the minister said that they might open the coffin lid to release the end of the shawl, that they found out what held it so fast.

There, inside the coffin, was the corner of the shawl, held tight in the bony fingers of the man who was buried there. It was the grave of the lass's lover whose drowned body had been washed ashore and buried by the villagers.

When the lass recovered from the fright of that terrible journey she went back to her own village again. But she wept no longer for her dead lover, since she had no wish to disturb him, lest he come and carry her off again.

The Flitting of the Ghosts

U P in the Scottish Highlands there once was a clan
of Scottish ghosts who were having a terrible time. A
raggle-taggle lot they were that had kept together, some
of them, for as long as two or three hundred years. Of
course, there were some whom one would consider
newcomers, but the important thing was that they all
belonged to the clan, which was why they all stuck to
each other like cockleburs to the wool of a stray ewe.

Not one of them could ever have been considered
respectable when alive and in his flesh. A randy crew
they all were, having been smugglers, pirates, catterans,
reivers, and followers of a number of equally disrepu-
table trades as men, and as ghosts they were as rackety
as they had been before they died.

They made their home in an old tumble-down castle near the sea, close to the place from which the family had originally sprung. The worldly clan was fast dying off, and those few members of it who were still alive had wandered far and wide. But no matter how far from home a clansman got, the minute he died his ghost would hotfoot it back to the castle, to take his place there with the rest. Although of late they were coming along fewer and fewer, still one or two would show up every now and then. As time went by, maybe the castle was getting a wee bit crowded, but none of the ghosts minded that. If anything, they liked it that way, because, being so numerous, they could kick up a fine old row when any curious mortal came poking about the castle. All the folk for miles around were so scared of the ghosts that not a body among them would come within sight of the place.

So there the clan were, having their pleasant little feuds and friendships, quarreling bitterly and making up joyfully, with never a dull day to fret them, as happy a crowd of Scottish ghosts as ever you'd hope to see.

Their troubles began when the castle was sold to a man who came from somewhere down below the border. A master builder he was, or so folk said, who made his living building grand houses for Englishmen who had the money to pay for such things. It wasn't that he wanted to live in the castle, Heaven save the day! But having an eye for business, he saw that the leaden roof and the fine old woodwork and stone would make the sort of building materials that he could use in his trade.

The builder moved in upon his castle with a crew of

his own workmen, Sassenachs to the last man, and without the least warning they all pitched in and began to tear the castle down.

The ghosts were terribly annoyed when the roof was suddenly snatched away from over their heads. But after it was gone, they found the floor of the attic would do very well for a roof, so the damage was not too bad. It wasn't until the walls of the castle began to come tumbling down about their ears that the ghosts were at their wits' end. The top story was gone, and the wreckers were starting to pry out the great gray stones from the walls of the next one, and it was plain to see that very shortly there would be naught left of the castle but the bare cellar holes and the empty moat.

The ghosts were fair distracted. They had not been standing about and doing nothing while all this destruction was going on. The minute the strangers appeared at the castle, they had mustered their forces and prepared to drive them away. But the worst of their tricks were no good at all. The poor ghosts raised a terrible racket, but the rumble of falling stones, the screech of splitting wood, and the thunder of crashing beams was louder yet, and easily drowned out the loudest noises all of them together could make.

They gibbered and mowed and made terrible faces, swooping down upon the workmen, thinking to frighten them away. If the men had been Scottish workers, the sight of a sluagh of ghosts coming at them might have put them to flight. But these workmen were not Scots. They were all Englishmen that the master builder had brought with him when he came up from England, and they were all much too practical and hardheaded to believe in ghosts. They did not shriek and take to their heels when the ghosts came at them. They just looked right through them and paid them no heed at all, except for remarking to one another that the plaster dust was awful thick in the air at times. A man could scarcely see through the clouds of it, they said. All the while, the castle walls were getting lower, day by day. At last, one evening, after the workmen had laid off for the day and had gone to their quarters in the nearby village, the old ghost who was chief of the clan gathered the ghosts together.

"There's naught that we can do here, lads," he told them sadly. "We must just be flitting away."

"Och, aye," the others agreed. "We must be flitting away. But where?"

Where? That was the important question. Where would these ghosts, who would soon be homeless, find a new home? The chief of the clan would not let himself be daunted. He had faced many a trouble in his life as a mortal man and had weathered every one of them. Would he not do the like now he was a ghost? To be sure, he would. So he called to him a spry young ghost and bade him go out into the world and find a place the clan could bide in, and not come back until such a place was found.

The young ghost set off at once on his search. It was no more than a fortnight before he came back again, looking very pleased with himself.

"I've found it!" he said.

"Where is it? Is it a castle?" the ghosts asked.

"A-weel, it is not a castle," said the young ghost.

The other ghosts sighed a great and doleful sigh that sounded like the wind blowing through dry leaves in autumn.

"Come now, do not fash yourselves," the spry young ghost said kindly. "If it is not a castle, I promise you it is no worse. A grand big manor house it is, with plenty of space within for all of us, forty or fifty rooms in all, to say the least."

The ghosts gathered hopefully about him, and he went on with his tale.

"It sets high on a crag above Loch Doom," he told them. "The only house, it is, between the fishing village of Dulldreary by the sea and the town of Grimbailey twenty miles beyond across the moor. There will be no neighbors to trouble us there because the village is a good five miles away. The road runs by the manor, but the manor house lies away from the road, and there are trees all about it that hide it well from sight. There it stands, alone and empty, just waiting for us to move in."

"A-weel," the old chief said doubtfully. "I'm thinking a place the like of that would be having a wheen of ghosts within it already. I'm not saying it would suit me to share a place with a pack of ghosts."

"De'il a ghost is there," the spry young fellow said. "Och, there's no reason why there should be. 'Tis no ancestral home. The man who built it lived in it less than two years. What with the fogs rolling in from the sea, and the mists rising up from Loch Doom, and the mizzle drifting down from the moor five nights out of seven, the place was so dank and chill he could not thole it. He packed up his goods and his family and moved away. So, you'll see, no one ever died in it by violence to bring a ghost there, and for that matter, no one ever died there at all. Except for spiders and mice and a rat or two, it's as toom as the inside of a drum."

"Och, my lad, you've done very well by us!" exclaimed the chief. "We'll all be off, then, to the manor house."

The chief had been a sea dog when he was living, and he was well pleased to find out that the clan could go by sea for most of the way to their new home, instead of traveling over moor and mountain making the long hard journey on foot.

Some of the clan went off to fetch the ghost of an old galley that haunted the waters of the bay, while the rest of them gathered up their gear, getting ready to flit.

Three nights later the ghosts who had gone to fetch the galley brought the shadowy old ship into a hidden cove, a mile or so below the castle village, and moored it there. When the ghostly galley was laden with their possessions, the ghosts went aboard themselves. Up came the anchor, and the galley with its load went slipping quietly down along the coast.

The night that the ghosts came ashore at Dulldreary, if the weather was not worse than any the village had ever seen before it was certainly no better. The fog rolling in from the sea was that thick that it could have been stirred with a spoon. A man coming out on his doorstep to have a look at the weather would not be able to see the house of his neighbor across the road. 'Twas not the sort of night to be stirring abroad in, and Dulldreary folk showed their good sense by biding indoors. The fishermen did not go out that night. Their boats were pulled high up on the shingle with the oars and boat gear carefully stored away, and there was no visiting that night around the village to *ceilidh* with friends.

Along about midnight, the ghosts' galley came creeping along through a solid bank of fog and tied up at the pier in the small harbor of Dulldreary. The ghosts landed themselves and their goods and set the galley adrift to go wherever it would, and then they shouldered their belongings and started up the road from the shore toward the manor house, five miles away.

The fog kept the villagers indoors, most of them being by now in their beds, but it did not bother the ghosts at all. They were all so lighthearted and frolicsome because they were near their journey's end that they could not contain themselves. Like lads coming out of school to begin their holidays they whooped, they shrieked, they whistled, and danced and sang. Dulldreary folk woke in their beds and shuddered to hear them.

"Have you e'er heard sie' a storm?" they said, pulling the covers about them. "Hark, now, to the terrible sound o' the wind!" And the fishermen's wives among them praised the Lord that their men had not gone to sea that night.

The happy ghosts did not care how much of a din they made. With the fog to hide them, no mortal eye could tell who they were or where they were going. Up the road they traveled, paying no heed to the five long miles. Coming at last to the manor house, they all went in and joyfully took possession of the place.

In the village at the end farthest away from the shore there stood two shielings, one on either side of the road. In the one on the left hand side a young fellow named Angus lived with his parents, and a young fellow named Fergus lived with his parents in the house on the right hand side. There was no harm in either of these lads, but they were both so lively and so full of curiosity that the whole village kept a watchful eye upon the pair. It was well-advised to do so, for if there was any mischief afoot, Fergus and Angus were sure to be in it and, most of the time, leaders of whatever was going on.

When the ghosts were rollicking through the village, Angus, wakened by the uproar, raised himself from his bed and crept to the window to look out and see what was causing the commotion outside. At the same time Fergus, in the house across the road, was doing the same thing. As the two lads peeped out the fog lifted a wee bit for a moment. It closed in again quickly, but in that moment Angus and Fergus caught a glimpse of what looked to be a host of men carrying upon their shoulders boxes, kegs, sacks, and bundles of different sorts. In an instant the fog had hidden the strange sight, but Angus and Fergus had seen enough to make them very curious about it.

There was a good bit of talk in the morning about the noise of the night's storm. The villagers were amazed that, with all the howling and whistling of the wind, there was not a sign of damage done.

Angus and Fergus kept quiet before their elders but later, when alone together, each told the other what he had seen.

"Storm!" said Angus, grinning.

"Wind!" said Fergus with a chuckle.

"Let the auld folk think as they please," said Angus. "We know what we saw."

"Och, aye, and we're not telling," Fergus said. "There was a terrible lot of men—"

"Hundreds of them!" said Angus. "All carrying boxes and the like."

"Smugglers!" Fergus agreed.

"Look, Fergus. Where would you say they'd be making for?" asked Angus.

"Making for? Och, for Aberdoom Manor house," said Fergus. "Where else?"

And it was to the manor house the two curious lads meant to go, as soon as they had a chance.

It was not soon the chance came, for it was the season for the herring run. Sure enough, the night after the big fog the waters were full of fish. The weather, though foggy, was not so bad that the fishermen could not go out, and every man in Dulldreary, Fergus and Angus among them, was needed to go out with the fishing fleet, night after night.

The run was over at last, and what with taking the fish they'd caught to the fish buyer and salting down those they'd kept to eat at home, to say nothing of cleaning the boats and mending the nets, the folk of

Dulldreary had had enough of fish for a while. The catch had been a good big one, and to celebrate it, there was going to be a grand *ceilidh* in Dulldreary at the village hall.

The night of the *ceilidh* the moon hung like a polished golden plate in the cloudless sky. There was not a soul in Dulldreary who bided at home that night. When the fun was at its height, Angus and Fergus slipped unnoticed away from the *ceilidh* and started up the road that led to the manor house.

The ghosts had settled in and were well-contented. They were having a *ceilidh* of their own, a housewarming you might call it. When Angus and Fergus turned from the road and started up the lane that led through the trees, they heard the sound of voices shouting, and music and laughter, coming from the house ahead.

They came up to the front door and found it standing open. No one seemed to be in sight, so the two stepped into the manor house hall. At one side there was a long dark passage running through the house. At the end of the passage they saw a light shining dimly where a doorway led into a room, and that was where all the din was coming from.

Angus started down the passage. "Come along, Fergus," he said.

"Och, I dare not," said Fergus, hanging back. "I'm feared o' smugglers."

"Och, weel, so am I," Angus said. "But come along anyway."

So they crept down the passage, keeping close to the

wall. The din grew louder and louder as they came near the doorway. They peeped around it to see what was going on.

It was the grand ballroom of the manor house, and Angus and Fergus saw at the far end of it a great long table stretching clear across the room. The place was none too bright, for the only light came from a row of candles down the middle of the table, but anyway they saw what looked like scores and scores of men gathered about the table, having a high old time. They were a strange looking crew to see and as wild as foxes, and they were feasting and drinking, dancing and singing, talking and laughing, till the rafters rang. There was even a piper or two blowing away.

The corners of the room near the door were dark, being too far away for the candlelight to reach them. Angus and Fergus crept into the nearest corner and crouched there to get a better view. There were things piled up on either side of them, so the lads were as well hidden as if they were in a cave. They watched for a while spellbound at the queer sights, then Angus, finding his eyes were getting used to the darkness, looked at the pile of things beside him, curious to see what was there.

There at his elbow was a great heap of leather bottles stacked up like the stones in a cairn. He poked Fergus in the ribs, and pointed a finger at the pile.

"Look ye," whispered Fergus. "Whiskey, I dinna doubt."

"Och, more like 'tis brandy the smugglers sneaked in from France," Angus whispered back.

"A wee bit of it would not be so bad," and he reached out and took hold of one of the leather bottles by its neck.

The bottle pulled from the pile dislodged all the rest of them and down they fell with a clatter, bouncing and banging on the bare board floor.

The company about the table stopped their carousing and turned about to stare at Angus and Fergus who stood, horror stricken, in the corner, Angus with the bottle still in his hand. His eyes and mouth flew open, and Fergus's did the same. They could look right through the men around the table and see the wall of the room beyond them!

"Ghosts!" screeched Angus.

"Smuggling ghosts!" shrieked Fergus. "Let us get out of here!"

The ghosts swooped down in a body, but Angus and Fergus were gone. Down the long passage the two lads flew and out the front door, clearing the front steps in one bound. The ghosts came pelting along after, but the lads were well ahead of them. Down the lane through the trees, and into the road, and on toward Dulldreary they sped. Luathas, the swiftest dog that ever lived, would not have outrun Angus and Fergus that night.

The ghosts chased them down the road for a mile or two but could not catch up with them, so at last they gave up and went back to the manor house.

Angus and Fergus kept up the pace for another mile, until they discovered their pursuers were gone.

"I've no breath more for running," Fergus panted,

dropping down under a hedge by the road, and Angus threw himself down by his side. They lay gasping and panting until they got their breath again. Then they sat up and looked wildly at each other in the pale moonlight.

"That would be ghosts, to be sure," said Fergus.

"Och, aye, indeed it would!" said Angus. "Smuggling ghosts, into the bargain."

"What's that you have in your hand, Angus?" Fergus asked.

"Och, this? 'Tis the bottle. Och, now! Did I forget to put it down when we left!" said Angus.

"Well, then," said Fergus. "Open it up! With all the running I've been doing and the shock I've had forbye, I'm needing a bit of a drink."

So Angus opened the bottle and it went back and forth between them. The very best of old French brandy was in it, and between the two of them they drank up every drop.

The *ceilidh* at Dulldreary village hall ended around about four in the morn, and dawn was getting ready to cry itself in when Dulldreary folk were settling down in their beds. There wasn't a body waking in the place when, an hour later, Angus and Fergus came roaring down the road. The two lads stood in the middle of the road shouting to all the folk of the village to come out and hear their news.

The villagers woke and leaping from their beds rushed out their doors, thinking the houses were on fire and the village about to go up in flames. When they found out it was naught but Angus and Fergus babbling of ghosts and smugglers, they turned in disgust and went back to their beds again, leaving the lads to their parents who put a flea in each of their ears for shaming them before the neighbors with their foolish tales. Folk would think they were daft, going on in such a way, they scolded, and sent the silly lads off to their beds.

But when the villagers had had their sleep out, they were willing to listen, and even paid some heed to what Angus and Fergus told them, although nobody was quite sure what it was all about. They were certain of only one thing: something very queer was going on at the manor house. The villagers were divided on the subject. Half of them said it was smugglers, bringing in wines and silks and the like from France or maybe Spain. There had been smugglers in their grandsires' day, so why not now? The other half would not hear to that. What would be more likely than a lot of ghosts in an empty old house left so long ago to itself?

In the end, both sides won, in a manner of speaking. Those who said it was smugglers sent for the King's Men to come and arrest the rogues for not paying their tax. Those who said it was ghosts got the minister to promise to go and exorcise them with his bell and his Book.

Back at the manor house the ghosts were in a terrible taking. Being discovered by two lads was bad, but the lads would tell about it all over the countryside and that would be a hundred times worse. After their defeat by the master builder and his workmen they doubted their power to deal with a horde of cotters and crofters and fishermen. They sat and keened like mourners watching over the dead. They had been homeless before. Were they to lose the grand big manor house, and be homeless again?

The old chief took his stand undauntedly. "Leave the greeting till later," he said. "It may not be needed at all. This is a time to do something helpful, not to sit idle, rubbing the tears out of your eyes."

He called the spry young ghost to his side and bade him go down to the village and spy on the folks, to learn what they were planning to do.

"Look to 't, lad, that none see you," he warned. "The sight of you would add to the trouble we have already. And hasten back as soon as you can."

The spry young ghost was clever enough to keep from sight, although the lack of anything much in Dulldreary made it hard to keep out of view. He lurked about behind outbuildings and boulders, and managed very well. What he heard sent him speeding back to the manor house.

"Did you see aught?" the old chief asked, and the ghosts crowded around to listen.

"Did I not!" said the spry young ghost. "The folk at Dulldreary were all of them talking about us and the manor house."

"Och, what would they be saying then?" asked the chief.

"Well, I heard some say that the King's Men were coming to haul the smugglers in the manor house off to prison."

"The King's Men!" said the chief. "That is no matter. We can take care of the King's Men."

"Aye, that we can!" the other ghosts said.

"Och, ye've not heard the worst o't," said the spry young ghost. "There are others who are coming up here, bringing the minister along to exorcise us with his Bible and bell."

"Och, that's bad!" said the old chief, and he turned paler than ever a ghost was before.

"Exorcise?" said some of the ghosts who had never had much schooling. "What would they mean by that?"

"That's what happens," the chief told them, "when the minister comes and reads from his Book and rings his bell, and says some hard words over a ghost. Then —Woosht! You're exorcised. That's the end of you!"

"But where do you go?" they asked, bewildered.

"Nowhere," the old chief said. "You're out like the flame of a candle when somebody snuffs it."

"I do not want to be exorcised," cried one ghost, and the others in chorus echoed his cry.

"Nor I!" the old chief said. "But before they do that, they'll have to find us. Come, now, let us make sure that not a hide nor hair of us will meet their eye."

Down in Dulldreary the King's Men had arrived, full of courage and both of them armed to the teeth. They headed the procession leading those who had held out for its being smugglers at the manor house.

The minister came after them with his Bible under his arm and his bell in his hand, and after the minister the rest of the villagers, being the ones who believed the manor house was lodging a sluagh of ghosts. And at the end came Angus and Fergus, scared but plucky, and as curious as ever about what was going on.

The night was misty and wet, with a bit of sea breeze behind them urging them on. Up the road the procession moved slowly, picking out the way by lantern light, for every villager brought his light. Up the five miles from the village they plodded, and up the lane through the trees, and came to the house, standing tall and dark and scarcely to be seen.

The King's Men went up to the big front door and banged upon it with their fists. They could hear the sound echoing through the rooms on the other side of the door.

"Open in the name of the King!" called out the King's Men. But no one opened the door.

The minister came up beside them. He was an old man, but full of fire and spirit. He, too, knocked on the door. He lifted his stern old voice and thundered, "Open in the name of the Lord!" But no one answered, and the door stayed closed.

Then, one of them laid his hand on the handle of the door and turned it. The door was not locked and opened readily. Into the hall of the manor house all the company crowded: the King's Men, the minister, the Dulldreary folk that believed in smugglers, and the ones that believed in ghosts, and Angus and Fergus at the end. They went down the long passage and came to the door of the ballroom, as Angus and Fergus had done before. They walked in, one by one and looked about them, and saw—nothing at all!

From the cellars to the garrets, in and out of every

room, opening every cupboard and press they went, searching the house from top to bottom and from end to end. They found an old empty rattrap in the scullery, and a pile of nuts that squirrels had stored and forgotten in the attic. They found an old broom, lopsided and worn, behind a bedroom door, and mice tracks and spider webs galore. But they did not find in all the forty or fifty rooms of the manor house, to say nothing of the attics or the garrets, even so much as one smuggler, or one lone ghost.

The King's Men were wild with rage. They hauled Angus and Fergus out from among the villagers where the lads had thought it wise to take cover, and started back to Dulldreary with them. All the five miles to the village the King's Men cuffed and cursed Angus and Fergus for bringing them so far on a fool's errand, while the minister followed close behind them, praying that the Lord would forgive them for telling such terrible lies.

The folk of Dulldreary had plenty to say about it to Angus and Fergus that night, and each of them had a thrashing from his father that neither would soon forget. It hardly seemed fair, for after all, the two lads *had* seen the ghosts. They had the leather bottle to prove it, and if the bottle had not belonged to the ghosts where did it come from? But the villagers were so angry about the lads' trick, as they called it, that Angus and Fergus never mentioned the bottle at all.

When the ghosts saw the lights of the lanterns fade and die away as the procession went farther and farther down the road, and no sound of tramping feet or of voices came up to them on the breeze from the sea, the ghosts climbed down from the trees where they had hidden themselves away, and gathering up their possessions from the bushes where they'd put them, they moved themselves and their gear back into the manor house.

Dulldreary folk lost all interest in the manor house, and Angus and Fergus had had enough of it to last them all the rest of their lives, so nobody ever went near the place. The trees grew up closer about it, and the bushes and brush grew taller and hid it, until a body going by on the road would not know it was there at all.

But the ghosts were canny. They took no chance of being discovered again and exorcised. When they wanted to have a *ceilidh,* they took care to hold their revels on nights when the sea fog rolled in from the sea, and the mists rose up from Loch Doom, and the mizzle drifted down from the moor, and only the fishermen, who had to, went out into the weather, and they, poor souls, went out to sea.

So forever after the clan of ghosts lived, undisturbed and happy in the manor house, and most likely living there to this very day.

The Auld Cailleach's Curse

W HEN the clans who supported the Stuarts in the Scottish rebellion of 1745 went out to fight for Bonnie Prince Charlie, the Laird of Kennaquhaur was among them, and after the defeat at the battle of Culloden he was lucky enough to get away uncaught. He and some of his clansmen took to the hills, and after dodging about to evade the English soldiers for some weeks, they managed to get to the coast and found passage to France.

All the Scottish lairds who fought for the Young Chevalier, Prince Charles Stuart, were declared traitors and outlaws, and their lands were seized under what was called an act of attaindre, which meant that the lairds were homeless, landless, and penniless. Even at that, the ones that got away were fortunate, because many of those who were caught were put to death as rebels. The demesne of Kennaquhaur was forfeited, of course, and a factor, or manager, sent up from London to take over the estates and run them to suit himself.

The London factor was a hard-faced man with an ugly tongue and a stone in his breast for a heart. Cruel hard he was, as Kennaquhaur folk soon found out.

There was a road running through the estate from one side to the other that folk had used for maybe a hundred years or more when going from Kennaquhaur village to the market town beyond. The factor was not going to have folk traipsing past his front door all the time, and he gave out word that anybody going along the road would be taken up and punished as a poacher. The penalty for poaching was severe, being at worst, transportation to the colonies or even death, and at best, which was bad enough, the slitting of a man's nose or the cutting off of his ears. With that thought in mind, a body would not dare to travel the factor's road, even though it meant going ten miles farther by the high road that ran outside the estate. Folk had seen so much trouble since the battle of Culloden that they were resigned to it. They went the long way by the high road without any protest at all.

But the factor was not through with his mischief-making. Where the road entered the estate on the side near the village, there were a few small shielings. The grandfather of the young laird who escaped had built them so that the old servants of the manor might have a place to bide in when they were too old to work. There were only a half dozen of them, and they were neat and well cared for on the whole. At the time the factor took over Kennaquhaur there were an old shepherd, beyond weathering wind and rain and sun, with his wife in one shieling, and in four others an ancient stable groom, a sewing woman whose hands were too gnarled and whose eyes were too dim for needlework, and there were two old serving women who had spent more than half a century serving the lairds and ladies of Kennaquhaur. And in the last shieling dwelt Auld Jeanie who had been nurse to the young Laird of Kennaquhaur and to his father before him. Here in this little shielan these old people were quietly and contentedly living out their last days.

So not only the folk on the Kennaquhaur estate, but those on all the other estates for miles around were struck with horror when they heard that the factor at Kennaquhaur had given the order that all the old people were to leave the shielings, and with only a fortnight to get out. There was naught that anyone could do to help them. Even the lairds who had not had any part in the rebellion were under the hand of the oppressors who had taken over the country.

"Where will they go, these old people?" the factor's wife asked him, only to be told by her husband that they could go to the devil for all he cared, as long as they got out. The factor's wife, poor lady, was too much afraid of her husband to say anything more, but she was not happy, you may be sure.

The good neighbors set about seeking shelter for the

old folk and found homes for them in the village and in the fishermen's dwellings along the shore. The fortnight was soon over, and when the last day came men from the village arrived, some with carts, some with barrows, to move the belongings of the poor old souls.

The factor was there, too, sitting on his great black steed, keeping a watchful eye on all the goings on.

One after another the shielings were stripped of their bits and pieces of household gear. The carts were loaded quickly, baskets of fowls were tied to the tops of loads, and what livestock there was in the sheds behind the shielings was tied on behind the carts. A place was found for everything—even the shepherd's old dog and the women's cats. Finally, all the cottages stood forlorn and empty but one. That last one was Auld Jeanie's, she who had been nurse to the last two Lairds of Kennaquhaur. She stood at the door, blocking the way against the kindly townsmen who were trying to get into the shieling to fetch out her belongings.

"You'll not be moving one stick o' my gear out, young Geordie!" she said to their leader. "My young laird put me in the house here when I grew too auld for work. The laird would be wroth, I tell ye, could he but know what this Sassenach upstart has done this sorry day! I'll nae be flittin'. Dinna ye think it!"

"Och, come now, mistress," Geordie coaxed. "My mither's got a cozy wee room for you in our ain hoose, and a warm nook by the fire is waiting for you. Let me but get your gear on the cart, and you and me'll be going hame."

"I'll nae be flittin'!" Jeanie said firmly.

The factor rode up to the door. "What goes on here?" he blustered. "Why have you not emptied this house, my man?"

Geordie looked up at him. "The auld cailleach does not like to leave here," he said. "Happen she could stay a wee bit longer? She'd gi'e ye no bother. She's awful auld to make sic a change."

"The devil take the stubborn old hag," exclaimed the factor. "Whether she likes to leave or not, she'll have to go. I'm going to burn down the houses."

"Come, mistress, *mo graidh*," Geordie coaxed. "You canna bide here. Come along hame wi' Geordie, will ye not?"

The old woman took a firm grip on the doorposts at either side. "I'll nae be flittin'," she said.

The factor alit from his horse and strode up to the door.

"I'll have no more impertinence from you, old woman!" he shouted. "Let this fellow in to bring your furnishings out, or I'll burn them with the house."

Auld Jeanie looked him straight in the eye. "I'll nae be flittin'," she said.

The factor, furious because she dared to defy him, caught the old body by the shoulder and, hauling her away from the doorway, thrust her aside so roughly that she fell sprawling in the middle of the road.

Young Geordie ran out in alarm and lifted her up, brushing the dust from her skirts. "Come away, now, come to the cart," he begged.

Jeanie set him aside, and turned to face the factor. She fixed her eyes on his, and he stared back as if unable to turn away.

"I lay a curse upon you, factor," she said, speaking not very loud but very clear. "I lay a curse upon you! Hark to me! As ye have sowed, so shall ye reap. Evil you have sowed and evil shall be your harvest. I lay a curse upon you that the day will come when you shall hunger, with food within sight, and you not able to touch it. You shall thirst with water near, and you not able to take it and drink. You shall call for help and because of your own folly no help will come. When that time comes you will remember this day."

"The old woman's gone mad!" the factor muttered, half to himself, and turned away at last. With a curse, he sent the man whom he had brought along with him to fire the other shielings but Auld Jeanie's house he himself set aburning, with all her little treasures inside. Jeanie turned her back to the flames springing up behind her. Leaning upon Geordie's arm she walked with him to the cart, and let him lift her up to the high seat. Geordie climbed up to sit beside her, and the little procession of loaded carts and barrows moved slowly down the road toward the town.

The factor glanced at his workmen, who had come to stand beside him in the road, and he thought they looked at him strangely.

"Ignorant superstition!" he exclaimed, and when they did not answer, he strode to his horse and mounting it, he rode away, leaving the shielings flaming high behind him.

Geordie's mother welcomed the old cailleach warmly. Geordie told his mother what had happened, but Jeanie had little to say. They put the old body into an easy chair in a warm nook beside the fire, with a tuffet to set her feet on, and a pillow behind her head. They thought she had fallen asleep and walked softly as they went about the house, but they need not have put themselves to the trouble. When they went to bid her come eat her supper, they saw that she would never awaken again.

"The poor auld cailleach," said Geordie. "What with the fire and the flittin' and all, 'twas too much for her."

"It was so," his mother said. "And her being so frail, forbye."

But then, as everybody said, happen it was best that it turned out that way. Jeanie could never have contented herself in any house but her own. And all her belongings gone—not so much as a kerchief or keepsake to bring with her. "Och," they said, "happen 'twas a mercy she did not live to grieve."

Early one morning in autumn, shortly after the burning of the shielings, the factor called for his horse to ride out and look about the demesne. The farm lasses were already out in the fields with their sickles, helping the men to harvest the golden corn. All autumn's loveliest coloring was beginning to show. Nuts were browning under the sun, rowan berries and haws red and bright in the hedges, and the early apples beginning to ripen on the bough. A man should have been happy in a world so fair to see, but the factor was not contented. He rode on and after a while came to the desolate spot where the ruined shielings were. He got down from his horse to look about the place. Where the road entered the estate a chain had been stretched across the way. A sign hung from the middle, banning the use of the road and warning all who came by of the penalty. The factor walked down to it, to make sure that the chain was fastened tight to the posts on either side. As he stood there he saw three carts laden with sacks of grain going along the highway below, and he grinned to think their journey would be ten miles longer now than it was before he had denied them the use of the road. He took pleasure in the thought because it showed his power.

But he had other things to think of than carts going to the miller. He turned back to the ruins of the burnt cottages and frowned. All this would have to be cleared away. It was a most unsightly mess. Clear it all away, he thought, and level the ground so that no trace of the houses would be left. He would have a big pair of iron gates put across the entrance of the road, and maybe a fence about the stretch of woodland at this side of the estate. There would be other clearances, too. He wouldn't touch the home farm nor the scattered crofts and grazing lands. They paid more than their keep. But there were cottages here and there in the wood, where laboring men and their families lived. Those houses—little better than huts, most of them— must be cleared away. They would have to be emptied and burned, as these shielings among which he stood had been. What the factor had in mind was that he meant to make a deer park, such as great gentlemen had in England. You cannot have people living in a deer park, frightening the deer. To the factor the deer were most important. The people would have to pack up and go. As a gentleman lived, so would he. Since he was sure the Laird of Kennaquhaur would never dare to claim his forfeited estates, the factor saw no reason why he should not be living there all the rest of his days.

He stood in the midst of the destruction he had caused and looked about him, at the jagged walls that remained, and the stones and bits of burned wood. His eye fell on the well in the garden of Jeanie's shieling, and then he saw the apple tree beside the well. The boughs of the tree were burdened with apples and every one was ripe and brightly red. The sun had not yet risen high and the fruit was still dew-pearled.

It was long since the factor had broken his fast and the apples roused his hunger. He would pluck himself half a dozen or so and eat them as he rode home. So he strode over to the well.

He reached up but try as he would he could not pick an apple. The fruit dangled just far enough out of his way to miss his fingers. There beside him was the well, and over it a cover of stout oaken boards. The well-curb was not high above the ground. Standing upon it he could easily reach some of the finest apples on the tree.

But though the wooden cover looked solid and strong, its appearance was deceiving. Years of dampness, winter frost, and summer sun had set the dry rot and wet rot working on it. Though the surface seemed sound, the wood below it had decayed and crumbled until the cover was like an empty shell. The factor, seeing only that the boards looked thick and strong, stepped up and onto the cover of the well. But the minute he put his weight upon it, the rotting wood gave way and down he crashed into the well—down—down— down. Shocked, bruised, and angry, he used what breath he could find to curse the mishap that had befallen him. But soon he gave up ranting, and began to think about getting himself out.

He tried first to climb out of the well, but there were no jutting stones or ledges that he could set his feet upon nor catch hold of with his hands, and the sides of the well, covered with the moss of ages, were too smooth and slimy to be grasped. Luckily, the water was not deep. It came only to his knees, so he was in no danger of drowning. But until someone came, he would have to stay, willing or not, in the well.

He called to his horse, but the creature did not come. He called for help; he shouted; he whistled; he yelled until he was out of breath. He grew thirsty, but he could not reach the water, nor bend in the narrow well to bring himself closer to it. After a while he became hungry. There were the apples on the bough above the well, within his sight but too far to be touched. He called again for help but nobody heard him and nobody came. He had only himself to blame, for no one passed by on the road he had closed.

It was then that the factor remembered the auld cailleach's curse, and thought of the water he could

80 .

not touch, the apples he could not reach, and the help that would not come, and shuddered with fear.

His horse had pushed its way through a gap in the hedge and wandered down to the high road, cropping the grass at the side. Some miles up the road it met with a band of tinkers and wandering horse copers on their way to a fair in the islands. Seeing a valuable horse roving about and no owner in sight, they took it along with them. They tangled its mane and muddied its sleek sides so that it would look more like their own nags, and hid it among the horses and cattle they were taking to the fair.

Night fell and day broke, and nights and days followed after, one after another. Wagons and carts rolled by on the high road outside the estate taking the long road, but no one came by on the road across Kennaquhaur. And there was no sound at all from the well.

The factor's wife was not worried when her husband missed his dinner. She was used to his staying away when he felt like it, sometimes for two or three days together, without letting her know. But when a week had gone by with no word from him, she began to fret. She was a gentle lady and terribly afraid of her husband, so at first she hesitated to start folk searching for him, lest he be angry with her, should he come suddenly home. But her kind heart gave her courage, so she sent word about that the factor had ridden out on his horse early one morn the week before and neither man nor horse had come back, so would they all seek for them, and if anybody should see them, let her know. The factor's wife was well-liked so what they would not have done for the factor, they willingly did for her. Men for miles around, from the estate, the towns and villages along the shore dropped whatever they were doing and went about seeking the missing man and his horse. Through the woods and glens they hunted, and over moor and bogland, and along the shore with its high steep crags and its bleak barren rocks and its caves with the sea waves curling and cresting around them. Anywhere a man could go on a horse they searched, but never a sign did they find. But folk have their own affairs to attend to, and cannot keep up a fruitless search forever. After a month or two, with the winter setting in, all agreed that there was no hope of finding where the factor had gone.

The factor's wife sent for Geordie and, knowing him to be honest and dependable, she put the home farm and crofts and all in his hands to look after. Then she shuttered and boarded up the big house and went off to London where she had kinfolk of her own.

Ten years went by, and then great news came to Kennaquhaur. Their laird—their own young laird, mind you—had been given a free pardon by the king! His lands had been restored to him and he was on his way home to take his place among his own folk, which was just as it should be. All the tenants and villagers turned out to get the big house ready for the laird. The boards were taken down, the shutters and doors and windows thrown open, and the house cleaned and polished inside from cellar to roof. The old house servants came trooping back, and soon the place had so much of its old air, one might have thought that time had turned back ten years and the laird away for the day.

The tenants turned out to welcome the laird on his return, and many were the tears of joy that were shed, and not by the women only. Indeed, the eyes of the Laird of Kennaquhaur himself were not dry.

For a week the laird was a very busy man. There were the books to go over with Geordie, who had been acting as factor all the long years. Then the laird had to hear all that had happened while he was away. Daily he went among his people or they came to him and, little by little, he gathered the story of the events of the years while he had been away. He heard about the burning of the shielings, and the closing of the road. "Geordie opened the road again, God bless him," they said, "as soon as the lady went away." But Jeanie and the old folk from the burnt shielings were all dead and gone now, and the factor had disappeared. It was all very strange, the way it happened. Auld Jeanie stood there and laid the curse upon the man, and within the month the man had vanished and neither hide nor hair of him nor his horse was ever seen again! There were plenty of folk who said Auld Clootie himself had carried the wicked factor and his horse away.

The laird rode out the next day to look at the place where the shielings used to stand. Time and the weather had worked upon the ruins of the old houses and all that was left were heaps of rubble and stones.

"Have the lads redd the place up, Geordie man," said the laird. "We'll make a bit of a green here, with benches where folk walking by may sit for a while and rest. Have them gather up the stones of the shielings and build a cairn of them. I'll be having a metal plate made to tell what happened here, and we'll fix the cairn in memory of what happened here."

The laird looked sadly at the deserted scene. "Och, Geordie," he said. "I'd not have had it happen, even if it cost all of Kennaquhaur to keep it from being done."

Geordie shook his head. "I was here when it was done," he said. "'Twas a wicked thing. Aye, a terrible wicked thing. Auld Jeanie died that night of the shock, ye ken."

"There's Auld Jeanie's apple tree, there," the laird said. "It could do with a bit of pruning. Och, the apples it bore were the best that grew in all the land. When I was a wee bairn in leading-strings I often had one of Jeanie's apples for a special treat. And there's that old well beside it. I've had no draught of water as clear and cold as that from Auld Jeanie's well since I had to run away from Kennaquhaur."

"The well is nae sae good, the now," said Geordie. "The lid's fallen in and the well's choked with twigs and leaves and the like. I've given it no care at all. Nobody ever comes to the place. Seems like folk took a scunner against it after the shielings were burned. When they come by on the road they hasten on, eager to get by, as if they feared some evil might be lurking here."

"A-weel, we'll soon sort that out. Get your men at it, to redd up the stones and have them look to the well," the laird told him.

"Aye, I will so," Geordie promised. "We'll be at it early the morrow's morn."

When the morrow's morn came, the laird, when he had broken his fast, sat down to work. He had thought to have a good long morning looking over the ledgers and papers for the ten years he'd been away. He had no more than started when word was brought to him that Geordie wanted the laird to hasten down to the burnt shielings because there was something there that he must see. So the laird laid aside his work and rode down to the place.

Geordie and some of his men were standing together by the well looking down upon something on the ground at their feet. When the laird alit from his horse and walked over to them, they moved aside, so that he could see what had held their eyes. Laid out upon the ground in the semblance of a man were the bones of a skeleton, and beside them a pitiful heap of tattered rags, buttons, and bits of leather, like snaps and belts, crowned with a heavy gold ring, with its stone dulled with dirt, and a silver-mounted riding crop.

" 'Tis the factor!" Geordie told the laird, in a whisper. "I knew him at once by his ring. I remember the way the diamond flashed when he laid hold on Auld Jeanie and tore her away from the door. Och, we hunted for miles around, all over the countryside, and all the time, God help him, he was here within the well!"

"I was out with the searchers," said one of the men.

"But we never thought it aught like this. We were looking for a man riding a great black horse."

"Och, aye," said another. "Who would ever be looking for a man on a horse in a well?"

"Auld Jeanie's curse!" said Geordie. "The auld cailleach's curse lay upon him. It must have happened the way she said. There he was in the well, and he could not get out. The well has gone dry now, but there was water in it then, maybe up to his knees. He could feel it, but when he grew thirsty, he could not get at it to bring it to his lips, because the well was too narrow for him to bend down or stoop. And when he grew hungry there were branches above him heavy with apples, all within sight, but he could not reach up and pluck even one. And he must have called for help, but no one would hear, for no one dared travel over the road that passed by the shielings, the road that he had closed himself. He was not a God-fearing man," said Geordie. "Cruel and hard he was indeed. But I could never have found it in my heart to wish him such a fate."

"Aye, so! It was the auld cailleach's curse," they all agreed. "Och, well, he brought it upon himself."

It was a strange thing that when the laird sent a gentleman to London to tell the factor's wife her husband had been found, she herself had vanished. Folk were vague about it; some thought she had gone to France; some heard that she had married again; some had almost forgotten her altogether. Geordie had no word from her after she went away, but as far as she had told him to do, he went on taking care of things.

The factor himself seemed to have no kith or kin to claim him, so the laird bade Geordie put the man's bones back in the well, and thus the well became his tomb. The stones of the burned shielings were gathered up, and the men built a cairn over the well with them, to mark his grave. A pleasant green was made, with flowers and young trees growing, and benches where weary foot travelers could sit and rest. Folk no longer hastened by nor feared that evil lurked in the place. The laird had a metal plate made and engraved to keep the memory of the burning of the shielings and of the auld cailleach's curse in men's minds forevermore.

Maybe if you should be traveling up in the north of Scotland some day, and take the road across the estate of Kennaquhaur, you will stop and read the plate on the cairn yourself, and if it is the right season, pluck yourself an apple from Auld Jeanie's apple tree. With the cairn to cover it, you'll not fear to be falling into the well.

The Shepherd Who Fought
the March Wind

IN the northern Highlands of Scotland, where the crofts are few and far between, there are shepherds tending their sheep on grassy braes, with only their faithful dogs to keep them company. Many of them will not lay eyes on the face of another living person for weeks on end.

The hours are lonely and long and tend to go by slowly, so the shepherds turn to many pastimes to make the time seem to go faster while keeping their eyes on their flocks. Some play on the fipple flute, amusing themselves by piping old songs or making up new ones of their own. But too much piping taxes the breath, and that's a fact.

Some of the shepherds find a big flat stone from which they can keep their sheep in sight while they dance upon it, practicing the intricate steps of the old Scottish dances: jigs, strathspeys, flings, and reels; humming to the tunes that spur their feet, with the hope that a prize will come to them when they compete with the dancers next Gathering Day. But a man's legs sometimes get awful weary. He cannot be at the dancing all the time.

Then there are some who read books, wanting to improve their minds, or maybe leaf through their Bibles for wisdom and consolation. But it is not too good to pass the time reading, because a man gets his mind so caught in a web of printed words that he can very well forget that he has sheep to tend.

Every shepherd has his own way of amusing himself in his hours of loneliness, but a lot of them will tell you that there is one way that is the best because it will not tax your breathing, nor tire your body, nor take your mind from your sheep. It's useful, forbye, because you've got something to show for it in the end. What would it be? Och, knitting, to be sure!

In the old days you'd find shepherds all over Scotland with their cleevs of woolen yarn, spun from the fleece of their own sheep, and their wooden needles, shaped and polished by themselves, sitting on their lonely hillsides with their sheep grazing peacefully about them, and all of them knitting away as if their lives depended on it. As they could knit, in a manner of speaking, with one eye on their knitting and the other on their sheep, nothing was neglected and their minds were at peace.

There was once a shepherd up in northern Perthshire who was a champion knitter, and took great pride in turning out vests and trews and hose galore. He was maybe a little bit dress-proud, and liked whatever he was clad in to be the best to be had. The things he knitted were unco fine. You'd have to pay a terrible price for the like, should you be buying them from a shop.

Do not think him a weakling because he was so good at knitting. He was not one of those wizened wee old fellows with a face brown and wrinkled like a crab-apple in a Hogmanay punch. This shepherd was a braw young callant with yellow hair bleached lint-white by the summer sun, and curling above his brow. His blue eyes were dark and clear and honest, and his mouth, when not smiling, was always ready to smile. If he was not handsome, he was good to look at, and that, for a man, is enough.

He stood well over the two-yard mark in height, and his weight was fourteen stone, every ounce of it strong muscle and hard flesh and sturdy bone. He could whip any man in Perthshire who would stand up to fight him, and maybe anyone in Scotland, too. He was proud of his family, himself, his sheep, and the land that gave him birth, and anything else that was his. In all the world or out of it there was naught that he feared.

His name was Murdagh MacAlister, and though he was young he already had a croft of his own, with a tidy wee shieling on it. The house lay at the foot of the brae where he kept his sheep. Above the brae was a high moor with bens beyond it, and to the side was a long deep lonely glen.

He lived alone but it did not trouble him, for he was out with his sheep on the hillside night and day. He had Balach the dog, the spunky wee sheepdog that guarded the flock for him, and he and Balach loved each other like brothers. With Balach the dog, and his sheep and his knitting, Murdagh made do very well. Every now and then when he felt the need of a change of scene he'd send for an old shepherd who had given up sheep tending as a steady job, but didn't mind taking on Murdagh's sheep for a day or two.

Then Murdagh would go down to his shieling and don his fine linen shirt with the ruffles and his finest kilt, and buckle on his wide leather belt. He'd put on his velvet jacket and his silver-buckled shoon, and fasten his plaidie on the shoulder with his brooch, arranging the folds so that they would show the tartan at its best. He'd hang his sporran from his belt and tuck his *sgian-dubh* into the top of his stocking, then he'd put on his bonnet with the badge at the side, and Murdagh MacAlister was ready for town.

He'd walk the long miles of the road and stride into the town with his back straight, and his chest out, and his chin up, and his hips twitching to give the proper swagger to the kilt, and every lass he passed would turn her head to look after him and sigh, and say, "Ochone! Were he but mine!"

For two or three days he would carouse about the

town, drawing after him a band of callants as wild and carefree as himself. Then, when the town was all but torn to pieces with their antics, he'd suddenly slip away and leave them. Back up the long road he'd go, to the shieling, lay off his fine clothes and put on his old ones, and go back to sitting and knitting and tending his sheep.

He'd sit on a stone that he'd always sat upon and he'd look about him, at the blue sky (when it wasn't murky) and at the green leaves fluttering on the trees. He'd look at the heather blooming on the moor above the glen, and at the bens, bare and blue and misty, beyond. He'd listen to the lark, rising to sing in the cool fresh air, and to the burn with its peat-brown clear waters chuckling over the stones. And Murdagh Mac-Alister would say to Balach the dog, "O Balach *mo chu,* what could be better than this?" And Balach the dog would poke his cold damp nose against Murdagh's hand to show that he agreed.

There came a day in March, with the lambing time over and the young lambs racing each other over the brae under the watchful eyes of their dams, when Murdagh sat on his stone in the sun knitting, with Balach the dog at his side. The day was mild and fair, with springtime slipping timidly but surely into the world. Murdagh's heart was easy in his breast.

Suddenly, down from the bens and over the moor the wild March wind rushed by, roaring through the trees and tearing the young new leaves off in handfuls, letting them fly behind him as he came. The lambs, greeting, ran to shelter themselves against the sides of their dams, and the ewes drew close together in a huddle to keep themselves safe.

But the March wind danced lightly over their backs and, racing up to Murdagh, seized the bonnet from his head and tossed it up toward the sky. Murdagh leaped up to catch it, but the March wind snapped it out of his hands and sped off with it so fast that Murdagh could not catch up with him. In a trice, the March wind and Murdagh's bonnet were out of sight.

It was only Murdagh's third-best bonnet, but it belonged to Murdagh and he liked it. He did not take it kindly of the March wind to steal it away. But it was gone and there was naught to be done about it. However, in March, a man was not wise to go out in the weather with his head uncovered. So Murdagh left Balach the dog to tend the sheep for a while until he went down to fetch from his shieling his second-best bonnet.

When he came back he sat down on his stone and went on with his knitting, and he had to knit twice as fast to make up for the time the March wind had wasted him that day.

The next day a misty rain kept falling and clouds hung heavy over the bens. Murdagh, to keep out of the mizzle, sat knitting in the wee doorway of the wee shepherd's bothan set against the wood. The March wind never came near that day.

The morn of the day that followed dawned bright and fair with the sky high and blue. The lambs played about on the green brae again and Murdagh sat knitting on his stone. He finished the stocking in hand and laid it in the flat creel that sat on the ground by the stone. There were three pairs of hose in the basket, now, and Murdagh was very well pleased. He picked up his needles to start to knit a new pair of stockings but before he could begin the wild March wind came whistling and shouting shrilly down from the bens. He hurtled over the high moor and took a wild turn through the glen, then racing up behind Murdagh, he snatched the second-best bonnet from Murdagh's head and carried it away with him over the moor and back to the bens again.

Murdagh was terribly put out about it, and Balach the dog was the same. Murdagh shook his fists and swore like a trooper, and Balach the dog reared up on his hind legs and bayed. Now Murdagh would have to go down to the shieling again, and what with all the wind's foolery he'd be getting behind with his knitting, to say naught of running out of bonnets. Still, a man could not go bareheaded in the chill spring air with always the chance of rain. So Murdagh left Balach the dog to tend to the sheep while he went down to the shieling to fetch his Sunday-best bonnet, which was the last he had.

It was a bonnie bonnet, and all but new, and Murdagh thought a lot of it. He set it on his head at the proper angle, and took a peek at himself in the looking glass to see how it looked, and it looked fine.

"This one," he said fiercely, "the March wind will not be getting from me!"

He went to the press and took out a linen napkin which he folded cornerwise. He put it on top of his bonnet, pulling it as tight as he could and knotting the corners under his chin. He jerked at the bonnet, back and front, but the napkin held it tight on his head. "Now let the March wind have a try at it!" he said, grinning. Then he went back to the brae. When he got to the stone he sat down upon it but he did not take up his knitting. Bolt upright he sat, with his shoulders square, and his arms folded on his chest.

Murdagh could hear the March wind howling and stramashing around the bens and the moor. He sat waiting for the wind to get sight of his bonnet and swoop down and steal it away.

It was not long he had to sit waiting. Down came the March wind, blowing with all his might, with the trees bowing humbly before him and the tall green blades of grass bending low. He came up behind Murdagh and gave a sharp tweak to the rim of the bonnet where it stuck out from under the napkin's edge. Murdagh's bonnet stayed as it was, for the napkin held it tight to Murdagh's head.

"Whee-e-e-e!" shouted the March wind, tugging away at the bonnet, and Murdagh, springing up from the stone, whirled himself about on the balls of his feet. He had his arms stretched out to keep his balance, and suddenly to his amazement he discovered that he had between his arms the body of a man, where he'd expected to find naught but air. He shut his arms and grasped the man as tight as he could. Murdagh could not see him, but he could feel the fellow's rib cage, and the flesh of his arms as he braced himself against Murdagh, trying to get away, and Murdagh could feel the beating of his heart against his own, as they grappled, breast to breast.

"Hiero!" thought Murdagh. "So this is the stuff the March wind is made of! Well do they call him the living gale!"

Murdagh's heart leaped for joy. Fighting with air was one thing, and a thing that could make a man unco uneasy, but there was not a man in the world, seen or unseen, that Murdagh was afraid of, and that he couldn't beat. Now that he had found out the March wind was a man, Murdagh would teach him a lesson he'd not soon forget.

The March wind writhed and twisted, setting his strength against Murdagh's, using every wile and trick he had command of, but he could not break Murdagh's hold. If the March wind fought hard to get free, Murdagh fought harder to hold him fast.

They struggled together on the brae, from the high moor to the kailyard above the shieling, and from the glen at one side to the wood at the other, and into the burn and out. The ewes gathered their lambs together and scurried with them to a far corner by the wood and crouched low with them under the cover of the bracken there. Balach the dog circled about the wrestlers, keeping out of the way but holding himself ready to dash in and help, should Murdagh give the word.

The joy of the battle coursed hotly in Murdagh's blood, and he shouted and laughed loud. He'd won many a fight before, but never one fought with an opponent he could not see! The March wind circled Murdagh's waist with his arms, trying to lift him and throw him to the ground, but Murdagh felt with his knee till he found the back of the March wind's knee, and tripped him so that he fell.

All of a sudden the fight was over, and there was the March wind lying upon his back on the ground, and Murdagh sitting on his chest with his knees holding the March wind's shoulders down. He had one of the March wind's wrists in either hand, gripping them tightly to keep them out of mischief, and although the March wind kicked and heaved it did him no good, for with the whole of Murdagh's heft on his chest, weighing him down, he was bound to stay where he was.

Murdagh shook the sweat out of his eyes and settled down to rest a bit. He could hear the March wind gasping and panting from the stress of the battle.

"Och, aye," said Murdagh with a grin. "Am I not panting a bit myself?"

He sat quietly until his breath came easy again, then he began to think of what he would be doing next. He could not just go on sitting there, holding down the March wind. A notion came into his head.

"O Balach *mo chu*," he said. "Fetch me the creel!"

Balach the dog fetched the creel with the three pairs of stockings in it that Murdagh had finished knitting. Murdagh forced the March wind's wrists behind his back and took both wrists into his left hand. With his right hand he took a pair of stockings from the creel and wound their double thickness around and around, binding the March wind's wrists together and tying the ends with a good hard knot. Then he felt around until he had the March wind's ankles and, taking care not to ease his weight from the March wind's chest, Murdagh bound the two ankles together with a second pair of hose from the creel.

"That will hold you for the time," said Murdagh, "but I can do better than that."

He took the last two stockings from the creel and knotted the ends together twisting them into a rope. With a quick twist he turned the March wind over on his face and put the stocking round his neck. Before the March wind knew what was happening to him, Murdagh had drawn his legs and arms together, up behind his back, and fastened them with the ends of the rope of stockings and tied them tight. Murdagh stood over him and laughed. "You'll blow no more for a while, you rogue!" said Murdagh. "That's a pickle you'll not be getting yourself out of soon!"

The March wind learned at once that the less he stirred about the better off he'd be. If he moved as much as a finger or a toe the cruel rope of stockings tightened about his neck so that he was all but choked to death.

Murdagh took the napkin from his bonnet and tossed it into his creel. He shook up the bonnet to put it in order, and set it back on his head.

"Och, now," he said to the March wind. "What will I do about you?"

"What are you going to do, Murdagh?" the March wind asked fearfully.

"Balach the dog and me were up by the bens one day, tracking a fox that was nosing about the hen run. We found a hole up there that led into a cave deep down in the ben. I'm thinking it would be a good place to drop you into. A good big boulder set across it to seal up the hole would keep you inside in case you were able to get yourself untied."

"Och, you would not do so!" the March wind cried in horror.

"Why should I not?" asked Murdagh. "We cannot have you lying here. The sheep would take fright at you, and maybe run away, losing themselves on the moor or in the glen. I'd be falling over you, not being able to see you. Sure, one or the other of us would come to harm. The best place for you is the hole in the ben, and when I get a bit of rest I'll carry you up and drop you in."

"Ochone! Ochone!" the March wind wailed. "Le-e-e-e-et me-e-e-e-e go-o-o-o-o!"

"I'll not do it," said Murdagh indignantly. "You've been naught but a vexation and a trouble to me in the past, and so you would be again if I should set you free."

And Murdagh sat down on his stone and taking up his needles and yarn he set to work at knitting the stocking he had begun that morn.

After a while the March wind said softly, "Murdagh?"

"Aye," said Murdagh.

"Murdagh," said the March wind. "I know a place over beyond the bens where two great kists full of gold and siller are hidden away. For more than a hundred years they've lain there, and the man who brought them there is long dead and turned to dust. Nobody knows the kists are there but me. Let me go free, Murdagh, and I'll blow both kists to you."

"What good would all that gold and siller be to a shepherd like me?" Murdagh said scornfully. "All a man needs is a good roof over his head, food to fill his belly, working clothes for weekdays and good clothes for Sundays. All these I have already, and my croft and my sheep, forbye. If there's aught else I fancy I'd like to buy, I'll have you know I'll get it for myself. I have a wee kist of my own, and though it is not full to the top, there's plenty of gold and siller in it to buy me anything I'm likely to want. Och, keep your kists for yourself."

Murdagh went on with his knitting, and after a while the March wind said softly, "Murdagh?"

"Och, aye," said Murdagh. "What would you be wanting now?"

"Murdagh," said the March wind. "Let me go free and I will blow fame and fortune to you. The king himself will give you his favor, and you will be a great laird in a castle, with servants to wait upon you. Would it not suit you fine to be proud and great?"

"Proud and great!" exclaimed Murdagh scornfully, with a flash of his eyes and a lift of his chin. "Och, ye great *omadhaun,* do you not know, then, who I am? Murdagh MacAlister, and my family goes all the way back to Alister Mor! There is royal blood in my veins, and there's no man in Scotland that is better than me! I'm that contented I'd not call the king my cousin. I'm very well suited the way I am. As for your castles, they are too big to please me. I'll take my shieling instead, and when the day comes that I need servants and cannot wait upon myself it will be because I'm dead and in my grave."

So Murdagh took up his needles and yarn and began to knit again. After a while the March wind said softly, "Murdagh?"

"Och, what now?" Murdagh said.

"Murdagh," the March wind said, "let me go free and I will blow you the bonniest lass in Scotland to be your own true love."

"Och, what sort of lass would it be that the wind would blow in?" Murdagh asked in disgust. "Why would I be needing anybody to get me a lass forbye? There are no bonnier lasses in the world than those in our own town. I can smile and crook my finger to any one of them and she'll come running to me. When I want a lass of my own I'll get one for myself. I'm weary of all your nattering. I'm beginning to feel like myself again, so we'll be going along to the ben and I'll drop you down the hole."

"Is there naught you would take at all to let me go free?" the March wind cried in despair.

Murdagh sat turning the question over in his mind for a long time while the March wind waited anxiously.

"If you play me false," said Murdagh at last, "I promise you that I will neither sleep nor eat until I catch you again and drop you into the hole in the ben."

"Ask what you will," the March wind said eagerly, "I give you my word."

"A-weel, in the first place," said Murdagh, "you must

bring back my two bonnets that you stole from me."

"That I will!" said the March wind. "And then?"

"Then," said Murdagh, "never again will you come roistering down upon us, bound upon mischief as you have so often done before. From now on you will leave the moor, the glen, the wood, and the brae, and all my croft, forever untroubled and at peace."

"That I will do indeed," the March wind promised. "So let me go."

Then Murdagh got up and went to the March wind. He untied the knots in the stockings on neck and wrists and ankles, and cast them aside. Murdagh heard the March wind rise from the grass with a great sigh and stretch himself. Then there was silence on the brae. Murdagh did not hear him go, but he knew that he was gone.

Balach the dog gathered up the three pairs of stockings and laid them in the creel, making sure that all six stockings were there. And Murdagh sat down on his stone and busied himself with his knitting again. Presently, the leaves rustled softly on the trees and there was a whispering along the grass, and into Murdagh's lap dropped his two bonnets—his third-best and his second-best.

One day, between spring and summer, the old shepherd came up to the brae and took the job of tending Murdagh's sheep, with Balach the dog to watch over shepherd, sheep, and all, and make sure all went well. Murdagh dressed himself in his best and went off to town. He strode down the high street, young and gallant and gay, with a high step and a swagger to his kilt, and every lass he met turned her head to look after him and sighed to see him pass by.

As he was going along he caught sight of a bonnie wee lass standing in the doorway of her father's house, and she was the one he had had his mind on, for a year and more. He was ready now to pick out a lass for himself, so he smiled and crooked his finger at her, and she came running to him. She followed him to the minister's house, and they were wed that day. Then Murdagh took his bonnie wee lass under his arm and they walked together up the long road home to Murdagh's shieling and to Balach the dog and the sheep on the brae.

Then there were three of them watching the sheep on the brae. There were Murdagh and Balach the dog, and when she had the shieling in order and her woman's work done, there was the bonnie wee lass forbye.

And after a year or so, there were four, because there was a wee bairn in a cradle beside his mother and father where they sat on the stone. Then, as the years went by, there were five, and six, and more, for a new babe lay in the cradle each year. How many bairns there were in the end, I cannot tell you, but there were a sluagh of them, all as healthy as ever you'd want to see. And on mild and fair days Murdagh and his bonnie wee lass would sit on the stone knitting, while Balach the dog kept one eye on the babe in the cradle and the other on the browsing ewes and the bairns racing over the brae with the young lambs.

It takes a lot of knitting to make all the vests and

trews and stockings and things needed to keep a raft of bairns warm and safe from the cold.

Sometimes, in the early spring, with lambing time over and the young lambs growing strong and frisking about their dams, the March wind would come slipping down from the bens, so secretly, so softly, that the bloom on the heather scarcely bent its head, the leaves scarcely stirred on the trees. He would lean to look at the flying fingers of Murdagh and his bonnie wee lass as they sat knitting, then he would move away to breathe gently on the sleeping face of the babe in the cradle, and to ruffle the curls of the bairns at play. Then stealthily, silently, the March wind would creep away from the brae, up the glen and over the high moor and back to the bens. Nobody ever heard him come, nobody ever heard him go, nobody ever saw him—unless it was Balach the dog, and if he did he paid him no heed at all.

The March wind never broke his word. The high moor, the glen, the brae with its bairns and its sheep, the croft with its wee shieling were left forever untroubled and at peace.

The Sea Captain's Wife

THERE is an ancient castle that stands on a dark crag above the sea on the northwest coast of Scotland. Ages of neglect, and winter's icy gales and summer's storms, have had their way with it, but still it rears its ruined walls proudly as ever it did when it was the grand stronghold it was built to be. The name of it has long been forgotten, and fishermen from the isles who use it for a landmark, when on their seal-hunting courses, call it *an dun na cuantaiche,* the Sea Rover's Castle. And it is the fishermen who through generations have kept the old tale of the castle alive, passing it down from father to son and from lip to ear.

At the foot of the crag there is a wide sweep of sand

and shingle half enclosing a wee bit of a harbor. The shore is bright and shining—*an traigh bhean,* they call it—and above the line of high tide, where the road comes down from the castle to the sea, a scattering of fishermen's shielings once nestled against the cliff. The shielings are long gone, and the fisherfolk who once lived in them are dead and forgotten. Nothing is left now but the white sands below and the old castle on its dark crag above.

Six hundred years have passed since the castle was built, and for a full half of them it has been abandoned and tenantless. No man's foot has trod its floors, no man's voice has echoed from its walls. The fox hunts through its passages by day, and the owl seeks its prey in its halls by night. Curlews call mournfully above its crumbling stones, and screaming sea gulls wheel around its ruined towers and return to the sea. The roof has fallen, the moat is dry, bracken grows among the stones of the courtyard, and there is an air of desolation over all, enough to chill a man's blood to behold it. Yet, the fishermen will tell you, there was a time when the castle was full of light and life. As the old story goes the time of its greatest glory was in the day of its last laird.

The last laird of the castle was young and handsome and gallant, in face and form and bearing all that a man should be. He was a sea captain and often away from home, but he had in his heart the true spirit of western Highland hospitality. His door was always open and a warm welcome awaited every guest. All in his household were instructed to welcome and provide for anyone who came to his house during his absence in the same way that they would have done if he had been at home. And so they did, indeed.

There was a day when the sea captain came home from a voyage, and went up to his chamber to change his travel-worn clothes for fresh ones before going down to greet the visitors who had come to the castle while he was away. As he dressed he talked to the ghillie who had brought him wood for his fire and water for washing.

"Who would my guests be?" he asked the ghillie. "Can you tell me who is waiting for me below?"

"Och, the usual run of folk from roundabout," the ghillie answered. "They having got word that you'd be returning during the day. Nay! I'm forgetting. There are two fine ladies from Edinbro' that are cousins of your own, or so they say. One of them has brought her young daughter along. I doubt they've been here before."

"Cousins?" the sea captain said. "Aye, then! That would be the Frasers. There were some of them from Edinburgh who were distant cousins on my mother's side, but the kinship is not close. Och, I've not laid eyes upon them since I went with my mother to visit them when I was a lad. I saw the daughter then." He settled his coat and shook out the lace at his throat and wrists, and finding himself garbed to suit his taste, he started down the stairs. As he went down he thought of the young daughter of his mother's cousin. He remembered her very well. A greedy wee dumpling of a lassie, that one had been, with tousled red hair. A whey-faced brat with her mouth always sucking on sweeties. She'd pawed him with her sticky wee hands, forbye! He shuddered at the thought.

Then he was down in the room where the company awaited him, greeting the gentlemen and making his manners to the ladies. And there were his mother's cousins, and one of them drawing forward a young lady by the hand and saying, "You'll be remembering my daughter, your cousin Catriona, will ye not?"

He stood, dumbfounded. This was no wee dumpling with sticky paws!

He looked, and saw a tall lass, a slim lass, as straight as a young birch tree. If her hair was red it was the red of pure gold, and her face was not the color of whey but so white and smooth that he thought it would put shame to the petals of the whitest rose that ever grew. He saw two eyes of gentian blue, two smiling rosy lips, and two rows of teeth like pearls. "This is all the beauty of Edinburgh!" he told himself. "All in one caillean."

She looked at him, and saw a big man, a tall man, with broad shoulders, and a handsome face. She saw a mop of black curls sweeping back from his brow, two bold black eyes with laughter lines at the outer corners, a firm mouth, a strong chin, and the proud air of a man who liked to have folk heed what he said, and to have his word obeyed. They stood there, silent for the space of half a minute, no more, looking at each other, and anybody seeing them would have said that nothing had happened at all. But in that short time he had fallen in love with her, and she with him.

Then he collected his wits and greeted her courteously, calling her "cousin" and bidding her welcome to his house. And she, composed and calm, replied, thanking him for his courtesy in receiving them.

That was where the trouble began. Because he had no right to love her. He had already given his heart to the sea. Nevertheless, he did woo her. He lilted to her, he danced with her, he sang to her, he talked to her, until he had her as tame as if she were a bird coaxed to his hand from its nest, and before spring turned fairly into summer they were wed.

He loved her, be sure, as much as he was able, but she doted upon him. The world held nothing for her but himself. Nothing else had value in her life. But she could never be more than second best in his life. His first love and his dearest love was the sea. Her heart nearly broke when she found it out, and they not more than two months wed. If it had been another woman he loved she could have fought for him, and no doubt won him. But how could one fight against the hold the sea can have on a man? Folk who knew him well told her that when he was but a wean in his nurse's arms he clapped his wee hands and leaped for joy to see the white-capped waves come rolling in. When he was a bairn he ran from home whenever he could, they said, to play around the boats and over the rocks with the fishing lads and lassies on the shore. When he was a lad half-grown he coaxed a boat of his own out of his father, and after that his days from morn to night were spent sailing along the coast, and his nights, as like as not, out with the fishermen until they came in from the sea with their fish in the early misty dawn.

Nobody had the need to tell her that now that he was a man, and master of a great ship, he loved the sea so dearly that he could not be happy long away from it.

So with their wedding day no more than two months behind them, the sea captain told his young wife that he was going to leave her and go to sea.

"But we have not been married long, *mo graidh*," she protested, unable to believe he meant it.

"Och, I'll come back," he said, laughing. "But I must go. I'll not be long away, *nighean mhúirninn*. A month, or maybe two." She stormed at him, she wept, she begged him to stay. But he only shook his head. "You knew I was a sea captain before you wed me," he told her. "Did you not expect that I would go to sea?"

"Do you not love me?" she cried.

"I love you, *nighean mhúirninn*," he said. But she saw his head was half-turned from her, and he listened to the murmur of the sea on the white sands below.

"You love the sea more than you do me," she said, and he said nothing. There was nothing he could say. It was true.

So a few days later he kissed her and bade her farewell, and went down to his ship and sailed off. And the sea took the ship in its arms and carried him far away.

In a month or so he came home, full of tales of adventures and bringing chests of booty taken in battles with the Portingales on the high seas. He poured out golden rings, fine jewel-set chains, earrings, wristlets, and pieces of gold in a bright shining shower, heaping them all, hugger-mugger, into her lap and laughing to see the fine show they made. But she stood up and let them all tumble to the floor.

"I care naught for these baubles," she said. "I had rather you were a poor ploughman and I your wife, to work and strive to make ends meet on a shilling a week—and keep you at home with me."

But she knew he would not stay. The sea would call to him and naught she could do would hold him beside her. So he went, and came back, and went again, over and over, and two years went by. She loved him no less. But she grew to hate the sea, and all things belonging to the sea.

Then one day he kissed her and bade her farewell as he had done so often before. But this time he did not return. He had been gone overlong and she began to grow anxious, leaning her breast against the window-sill, and watching daily and hourly for sight of his ship.

Then, a messenger came riding in with word that her husband the sea captain would never come back again. The messenger was not able to say how or when her husband came to his death. The captain of another ship, coming into port at Greenoch, had sent the messenger to her with the news. He thought something had been said about a sea battle, and a great storm, but what it was all about he himself could not say. All he knew certainly was that her husband was dead.

The captain's wife nearly went mad for grief. She shut herself in her chamber and would let no one come near her to console or advise her. The guests in the castle saw that she wished to bear her sorrow alone, and went quietly on their ways. They were uneasy at leaving her, but what use was it to stay? All their pleading would not bring her out of her room nor persuade her to open the door to let them come in. She did not want them, it was plain to see, so they could do nothing else but go.

When they were all gone she came out and for a day or two went here and there about the castle, and the servants, seeing her in her deep black velvet gown, with her face so white and her hair flaming out above it, thought she was far more like a sea fairy than a mortal woman. There was something fey about her, and it distressed and frightened them.

Then she called the servants together, and after paying them handsomely, she bade them go and seek to work elsewhere. They were unwilling to leave her alone in the castle, but she spoke brusquely and told them there'd be naught for them to do. She had a mind to shut the place up and go away herself, and she'd not be coming back in a hurry—if she ever came back at all— so they must go quickly. None of them dared gainsay her then, and within a few days the last of them had departed and she was alone in the castle. But she did not go away. By night and by day she stayed, brooding over her lost love, and the sound of the sea was in her ears all the days and all the nights of her life.

Then one day, as the sun was sinking into the far-off western sea, she looked out of the window and saw that a great ship was moored in the little harbor, riding at anchor on the gentle swell of the waves. She knew it at first glance, for if she had seen it once before she had seen it a score of times, bringing her husband home or taking him away. She could not bear the sight of it, for she knew it would never again feel the tread of his foot upon its decks. How and why the ship was there at its mooring she did not ask herself. She turned quickly from the window and did not look that way again.

Then she heard feet tramping the stony road that led up from the shore. She stood at the door and looked to see who came. Three seamen came trudging up to the castle and, as they drew near, the captain's wife saw that two of them were well-seasoned sailors with weatherbeaten faces and grizzled hair but the third was a fresh-faced, rosy-cheeked young lad, who looked hardly old enough to have got his sea legs under him yet. Each seaman carried a sea chest upon his shoulder, and they came steadily up to the captain's wife, where she stood at the door. They greeted her respectfully and, without replying to them, she beckoned them into the hall, standing aside to let them pass. They set the sea chests upon the great table that stood in the middle of the hall, and turned to face her, and then she spoke to them. "Why have you come here?" she asked.

"The captain said that we should bring the ship and the treasure to you, my lady, and so we have done," the oldest of the three sailors said.

"A ship and treasure!" the captain's wife said scornfully. "What am I to do with such things? I have no use for them at all. Why did you not bring my husband back to me?"

"That we would have done if we could," the seaman told her. "Och, the battle was over, and we were well away, but a great storm came up, with the winds blowing wild and the waves high beyond believing. Then the sea came up over the deck and carried the captain away. We tried to keep him with us, but our strength was nothing against the sea."

"So you let the sea take him," she said.

"We could do naught else," the seaman said.

She turned, then, and threw back the lids of the chests, and fingered the treasures within them, the pieces of gold and the jewels, and as she let them slip from her hands she had, in her inner heart, a feeling that these men were to blame in some way for her husband's death. She resolved that she would have their lives in payment for his. She shut the chests.

"Well, then," she said, "since you are here, you must have food and drink to refresh yourselves, and after a while I may have a task for you to do."

She led them to the guard room of the castle and bade them seat themselves at the table there. Then she went back and forth, bringing bread and meat and cheese from the larder and setting it on the table, and she fetched wine for them to drink. But before she brought the wine into the room she put into it a drug that would put them fast asleep.

They ate and drank, and she sat a little apart from them, watching while they made their meal.

Soon the drugged wine began to make them drowsy. They yawned and rubbed their eyes; their hands grew clumsy and fumbled with their food. Then, almost at the same moment, slumber overtook them, so that they lay soundly sleeping, with their heads upon the table by their plates. The captain's wife rose from her chair and looked about the room at the thick stone walls and at the iron-barred windows, and at the heavy oaken iron-bound door. Out of the room she went, and shut the door and locked it, and took the key away from the lock.

She carried the great iron key to the edge of the crag that loured above the sea, and standing there she threw it with all her might far out and into the waters below.

She turned then and went back and sat herself down beside the table where the three chests of treasure stood. The seamen would never leave the guard room, she said to herself. The walls were thick, the iron bars were strong, the door would stand firm against the battering of an army. If any of the sailors came from the ship to seek their shipmates, they could not open the door without the key.

As she sat there brooding over her revenge she caught the sound of someone moving near the open door. She turned to look, and there in a band of moon-light she saw her husband, standing on the sill. She sprang to her feet, believing for a moment that he had come back to her alive. Then she saw the cold sea water running from his clothing and his hair, and strands of bright brown seaweed clinging about his arms and neck. And when she looked into his face she saw that there was no light of life within his eyes. But it was when he spoke that the blood chilled in her veins, for there was the coldness of the dead in his voice.

"Oh, my poor foolish one," the sea captain said, in pity and in scorn. "What harm have my good sailors done you, that you desire their death? They are honest men, and faithful in carrying out my orders. You should have rewarded them and sent them on their way."

Then the madness that had been upon her, and made her plan the cruel deed, left her and she was sorry and ashamed of what she had done. "I have been wrong," she said. "Oh, what now can I do?"

"Open the door," he answered gently. "Open the door and let them go."

"That I cannot!" she cried. "May God forgive me! I threw the key into the sea."

"That is why I came," he told her. "See, now! I have brought you back the key."

And he held out his hand to her, and in it was the key to the guard room door.

She went and took the key in her hand, and it was cold and wet, but she rejoiced to have it back again, and her heart clear from the evil she had planned.

"I will do as you say," she promised as she took the key. Then she saw that he was turning away from her, to leave her, and she cried quickly, "Oh, do not go away! Stay with me, my own love."

But he only said, "Listen!" And she listened. At first she heard nothing. Then she heard the sea waves rolling upon the sands of the shore, and it seemed to her ears as if the surge of the sea was calling, "O co-o-o-ome, O co-o-o-ome." And she knew that he would go.

"Oh, do you not love me, *mo graidh?*" she asked in despair.

"I love you, *nighean mhúirninn*," he answered. "But I must return to the sea."

The hot tears rushed to her eyes and blinded her, and when she was able to see again, there was naught in the doorway but a pale band of moonlight. He was gone.

When the first flush of dawn showed in the east the captain's wife took the key and went to open the guard room door. The seamen still lay sleeping, but she went from one to another until she had them all awake.

"Come, now!" she told them. "The moon is breaking and there is need for haste."

When they came to her in the hall, she asked them, "Do you love the sea?"

"Would I follow the sea, if I did not?" the oldest of the three replied.

And the other man agreed to what he said. "I could not live away from the sea," he said.

"And you?" she said to the young lad. "Do you love the sea?"

"I do not," the lad replied. "I love the land. I had liefer be a crofter or a shepherd, by far."

"Och, the lad is daft," the older men told her. "He'll never make a sailor, though he follow the sea for four score of years."

"Well, let it be," she told them. "He shall stay here with me for a while, but you sea lovers must go back to the sea."

Then she told them what she had in mind. These two

who belonged to the sea, and loved it, as she could tell, must take the captain's ship for their own, and sail it wherever they liked to go. One of the chests of gold they had brought was to be theirs, as well. They cried out against it. It was too much, they could not take so much, they told her. But she beat down their objections with words of her own. What good was the ship to her? Had she not houses and lands and a storeroom full of gold and treasures of all sorts? One small chest of gold would never be missed. Besides, and let them take this to heart, it was by her husband's orders that she was doing what she did. Would they have her disobey her husband's wishes? He himself had told her what she had to do. At last they gave in, and took back the ship's papers which they had brought, and she made out another paper for them to prove their right to the ship.

"Come, now! Make haste!" she bade them. "Take the chest and go! The tide will soon be turning, and it is not going to stand still to wait for you!"

When the two older seamen had gone and the captain's wife and the young sailor lad were alone, she said, "How does it happen that you are a seaman, since you do not love the sea?"

"Och, well," said he. "My father and my grandsire and all the men of my family have been seamen, so when I was old enough my father sent me to sea."

"Why did you not find a plow to follow, if that's where your fancy lies?" she asked.

"Och, one needs money to be a crofter. Our folk are

poor folk and money is hard to come by," he told her. "And it was the luck of my life for me to find a place on the captain's ship. A better master never drew breath. I'm thinking it would have been beyond bearing to have the ship out again, now that our captain's gone."

"If you had a bit of money of your own could you find a place on the land for yourself?" the captain's wife said.

"I could," the lad told her. "My *oide,* my godfather, has a very good croft, and not a small one either. If I brought a bit of money along with me he'd take me in with him, and be glad to do so. He has no son of his own, and he cannot bide the sea!"

"All well and good!" said the captain's wife. "Now you must do as I say. In the paddock behind the stable there is a little black mare. You'll find a saddle for her hanging on the stable wall. You may have her, if you will promise that she shall never draw plow or cart, but carry you to town or to church. Saddle her and bridle her and fetch her to the door. Then you shall have the other chest of gold, to start you out with your *oide* on his croft."

He could no more change her mind than the two older seamen could, so in the end he went and got the mare.

When he came back, she smiled to see the joy that lit his eyes. "Take your chest now, laddie," she said, "and go. And may good health and good luck be with you all your days."

She went out before the castle and stood there where the road on one hand led downward to the shore and on the other hand led inland away from the sea.

She looked to the right, and there was the ship going out in the mid-morning tide to the open sea. Proud and stately, the vessel sailed, with the freshening wind in her sails and the full tide under her, and with her crew at work in her rigging and her two captains on her deck.

"May God help the poor souls," said the captain's wife, "for nobody else can. I doubt not the sea will get them in the end." Then she turned to the left, and there was the young lad riding along the road that led away from the castle and the sea. He sat proudly on the wee black mare with the chest on the saddle before him, and when he came to the bend of the road that would take him out of her sight, he halted for a moment to turn and wave good-bye.

"Praise be to God! The sea will never get that one," the captain's wife said.

So now they were gone. The lad had turned the bend, and the road was empty. The ship had sailed around the headland and could not be seen.

"I have done as my love bade me, and rewarded his honest seamen and sent them on their way," said the sea captain's wife. "Now what is there for me?"

She looked again and there was the sea, dimpling and smiling in the golden sunlight, murmuring softly on the silver sands. And she knew that there was nothing at all left for her because the sea had stolen her husband away and would never give him back again.

Slowly, sadly, the sea captain's wife went into the castle and, picking up the last chest from the table, carried it with her to her bedchamber upstairs.

And since there was nothing left for her in this world worth having, she did what the valiant women among her forbears would have done when faced with defeat, in the ancient times. With great care she attired herself and made herself fair to see. She dressed herself in the white satin gown that she wore on her wedding day. Then she opened the chest and, taking out the costly booty of her husband's last battle at sea, she began to deck herself. She put rings on every finger, set eardrops in her ears, hung jeweled chains about her neck, and clasped jem-studded bracelets around her wrists. Gold, and diamonds and rubies, emeralds, and precious stones of every kind shone and gleamed and shimmered in the shaft of sunlight that came through the open window of the room. She set a golden coronet upon her red-gold hair, and stood forth, beautiful and resplendent as a queen. And with the calm dignity of a queen, she laid herself down upon the silken coverlet of her bed, and her heart broke at last and she died.

It was a distant cousin of the sea captain who inherited the estate and the castle, since the captain had no son of his own to leave them to. But no one was ever able to dwell in the old castle after the day the sea captain's wife died. Not that they did not try, but none of those who attempted to make a home there could bear the way the restless spirit of the beautiful unhappy wife of the sea captain ranged through the castle calling her husband to come back to her from the sea.

The folk in the fishing village that once stood at the foot of the cliff beyond the white sands used to hear the calling too. The wives complained that the eerie sound of it woke the bairns of nights and gave them all a fright. The fishermen who belonged to the village said it made their blood grue to hear it, and they out on the sea in their boats at night paying out their nets. So at last the men of the village went to the laird on one of the islands—Barra, I think it would be—and got leave to come and settle there and make a new home for themselves and their families. It was a far distance from the castle, so they could live untroubled there.

The shielings they left stood empty and forlorn above the silver sands. But as years went by, sun and wind and weather had their way with the village as they did with the castle on the tall gray crag above. Then, one spring, a great high tide dashed over the shielings and washed them all away.

Now there is nothing left but *an traigh bhean,* the white sands, the dark crag, and the ruined castle, to mark the place.

That is the story the fishermen will tell you about *an dun na cuantaiche.* It was all so long ago that it happened, they'll say, back in their great-great-grand-sires' days. But they know more than they have told you, as you can see by the uneasy look on their faces and the shifting of their eyes. And if you press them, they'll tell you what they have not told you before. They've heard the call themselves.

Many a still night, coming home from fishing, when the sea is calm and the winds blow soft and low, they have heard the voice of the sea captain's wife crying out from the castle as they sail by. Then, from somewhere in the sea, they hear the sea captain reply.

"Do you not love me, *mo graidh?*" she cries.

"I love you, *nighean mhúirninn,*" he answers.

But between them forever, keeping them apart in death as in life, is the sea captain's first love, the sea.

The Man Who Missed the
Tay Bridge Train

MANY a queer tale is told about ghosts and
witches and demons and suchlike things, and what
truth there is in them only the folk who tell them
know. But there is one tale about a happening that
was not ordinary at all, and the old man who tells it
can vouch for it because he was acquainted with the
two men it happened to, and when he was a lad, it
was one of them who himself told the old man how it
came about.

There were two crofts lying side by side on a Scottish hillside, and the families who lived upon each
croft were not only neighbors to each other but very
close friends, being cousins two or three times removed.

Upon a frosty autumn night there was a bairn born to each crofter and his wife at each of these crofts, and a messenger was sent out from each house to inform their neighbor of the event. The two messengers met each other halfway in their journey across the fields and, upon comparing notes, discovered that the two babes were not only born upon the same day, but at the selfsame minute of the selfsame hour. And that was a strange thing, to be sure.

The two bairns thrived and were duly christened Robert and Thomas, for the two great Scots, Robert Bruce and Thomas Randolph, heroes of Bannockburn, but Rab and Tam were the names folk always called them by. Whether it was because of the coincidence of the time of their births or because of some special affinity between them, as soon as they were of an age to play about they were always to be found together. Own brothers could not have been closer to each other in affection than wee Rab and wee Tam.

When they grew a bit older they went to the village school together, with their pieces to eat at midday in their pockets and their satchels holding their school books hung over their shoulders. From the village school they passed on to the grammar school in the market town beyond the village, traveling the miles there and back on their shaggy moorland ponies, side by side.

Rab was the first son in a family otherwise all lassies, and Tam the least one a family of seven sons. For those reasons the two laddies were maybe indulged more than they might have been in any other case.

They both were let follow their own inclinations as far as the spending of their time was concerned, so after school and on holidays they roamed together over the hills and moors and through the glens and corries. They tickled the laird's salmon and snared his hares and baited his gamekeeper. They were an annoyance to the gentry for miles around, raiding their orchards and coaxing their dogs away to join them in their fun. They kept the sedate and sober villagers' heads shaking in reproof at their antics. But there was no harm in the two lads at all, and if their goings-on now and then gave a bit of bother to their parents, it was never serious enough to keep the old folk from sleeping sound of nights.

Their parents, though thrifty, were far from poor, so when Rab and Tam told them at the end of their grammar school days that they had it in mind to go to the high school at Aberdeen, there was no great objection made.

"Education never hurt any man who was willing to take it," Rab's father said. "Even if it is Rab's lot to be a crofter like me, it will help him later if he learns to keep his brain exercising itself as well as his brawn."

Tam's father was willing enough, for with six sons older than Tam to help him, his youngest could well be spared to take up any profession he chose.

So, still together, the lads went off to the high school where they spent the next four years, sharing the same classes, the same books, the same studies, and the same rooms, and in the course of time grew up to be well-behaved and reliable young men. When they had finished at the high school, they went back to their homes, and to the hills and moors and glens again.

But there was a difference in these holidays for, at the end of them, they would part. Rab being the only son of the family would stay behind to prepare himself to take over the croft when his father laid his work aside, while Tam, who was not needed at home with a raft of older brothers, would go to the university to study law.

It was the first parting the two lads had known since they were babes in their mothers' arms. In all the years they had never been away from each other longer than the space of a night's sleep. Being Highland men, they were not prone to make a show of their feelings, but their hearts were sore when the time came to say good-bye. Rab, who had come to the town to see Tam off, stood with him, waiting for the train.

"A-weel, Rab," Tam said, "the train will be coming soon, now."

"And so it will," said Rab. "It's whistlin' up beyond the bend."

"Och, well, I'll come home for the Hogmanay, and happen I'll write now and then," said Tam, taking the hand his friend offered.

"So do," said Rab.

Then as the train came down the line and Tam picked up his bag, Rab said, "Tam!"

"Aye?" said Tam.

"Look ye now," Rab said. "If you're needin' me, dinna fash yourself. I'll be with you as soon as I can."

130.

"That I know well, Rab," said Tam. "Och, aye! And if I'm needing you I'll send word."

"Even without it," Rab said, "I'll come."

Then the train arrived, huffing and panting, and what with the hurry and flurry of finding a place in a carriage and getting himself aboard with his luggage, Tam had time for no more than a hurried farewell.

So Tam was whirled off on the first lap of his journey toward the university, and Rab walked back to the inn and got the wee pony and cart that had carried them to the town and drove back home alone. But both of the lads were thinking alike: "A-weel, we'll be meeting again at Hogmanay."

Hogmanay, as the Scots call the New Year celebration, is the greatest festival of the Scotsman's year. All the other days in the whole twelve months are colorless beside the joys of Hogmanay with all its feasting and fun. King Charles II made an attempt to bring Christmas into favor again in the land of his forbears but met with no success. The Scots would have naught to do with Christmas and held fast to their Hogmanay.

So the thought of it was in the mind of each lad as miles lengthened between them, and it helped a bit. The parting was not forever. Only till Hogmanay.

Even at that it was cold comfort, because Tam left at the end of August and there were four months to get over before they would meet again. But the months would be busy for both of them and that would help to make them pass.

The work of a crofter begins at the first crack of dawn and ends with the gloaming, and when he has cleaned himself of the soil of the day and eaten his supper, he is ready for bed and sleep. Rab was often lonely but he was not one to slack his work and use the time for brooding. He pitched in and worked all the harder to drive his cares away.

"Look ye!" said his father one day to the plowman. "Our Rab is going to make the best master the croft has e'er had yet."

Tam was busy enough. His studies filled much of his time and gave him little leisure. But, in a way, he had it worse than Rab. Tam was in a strange place, with strangers all about him, while Rab was at home amongst his own folk. But since there was no cure for homesickness but a large dose of home and that he could not get, Tam howked into his books with such a right good will that those wise men set over him to keep an eye on his progress, told each other: "That lad is not a dullard!"

"He is not, indeed. Mark my words, the world will hear of him one day."

September passed at last, and then October, and November, too, and at the end of the first week in December, Tam wrote to his mother and to Rab to tell them that it would not be long before they'd see each other again for he would be coming home for Hogmanay, according to his promise.

"I'll be home a day or two before, maybe," he wrote to Rab. "The weather is mischancy at this season of the year, so I'm leaving a few days early to give myself plenty of time in case bad roads hold me back on my way."

He was not surprised to have no answer to his letters. After all, in little more than a fortnight he'd be starting home. But as the chill December days went by he had an urgent feeling that he should put everything else aside and go home at once. It was all he could do to keep himself from packing his bag and taking the first train he could get. He put it down to being homesick.

"Och, I'm daft," he said to himself. "I've put up with it for four months, as it is. Can I not bear it for the ten days that are left?"

So for ten days he bore it, fighting against an instinct that urged him to go home. The day of his departure came at last. It was a dark and drizzly day, with clouds hanging low and the western sky showing a queer dull shade of yellow slashed with streaks of green.

Tam came home in the afternoon to pack his bag for his journey. As he walked up the hill to his lodgings he could hear the wind whistling high above his head. Now and then a gust of it would come down to earth, setting the dustbin lids a-rattling, buffeting folk who were hurrying toward the shelter of their homes and pulling their clothes about, then darting off high into the sky again.

Tam turned in to his own front door, and just as he stepped into the hall the rain came down on the trail of the wind, falling in sheets that seemed to stack against each other like panes of glass.

"Whew! What a night!" he said to his landlady, who

had come into the hall to set a lamp upon the table by the wall.

" 'Tis that," she agreed. "Run along upstairs, now, and get your wet things off, and I'll bring you a good hot cup of tea."

Tam went up to his room and, having got himself ready for his tea, he drew out his bag and began to pack it.

His landlady came into the room with the tea tray in her hands just as he finished packing. "Och, now," said she. "I was just saying today to Mrs. McNeil next door that my lodger would soon be going to his hame for the Hogmanay."

"That I am," said Tam, smiling at her as he shut and strapped the bag. "I've been wanting to go so much for the past two weeks that it's been all I could do to keep myself from leaving any minute. But now that the time has come for me to go, I do not feel something at me, trying to force me to go the way I did. I'm just glad I'm going, of course. But that's all. Is that not strange?"

"You're young yet," his landlady said, "and not used to being from home. I was brought up in the Islands and married a mainland man. I mind how I used to wish sometimes at first that I was a sea gull, to have wings to take me home again, but after a while I got used to the town here, and I did get home for a visit now and again. To tell the truth, when my husband died, I was so used to the mainland that I did not go home to stay, although there was naught to stop me. I go home to see my own folk now and then, but only to visit. I would not like to stay. Happen it will be the same for you."

"Maybe it will," said Tam, finishing his tea and laying his napkin on the tray.

His landlady picked up the tray to carry it downstairs again. "Have you coals enough for your fire?" she asked. " 'Tis growing cold outside, and you'll need a good fire if you're minded to work late over your books."

"Not tonight," Tam told her happily. "I'll need no fire at all. I'm leaving tonight for home."

"Mercy on me!" cried the landlady, nearly dropping her tray. "I did not think it was tonight you were going! Why, you'll never be going out in such weather, what with the wind and the rain and all!"

"I will," said Tam. "I'm taking the Tay Bridge Train tonight. I dare not wait over until tomorrow because the roads will be bad at the other end of my journey, and if I leave myself short of time I might not get home for Hogmanay."

The landlady shook her head. "I do not like it at all," she said as she carried the tray away.

Tam put on his hat and his overcoat that had been drying before the fire. He came down the stairs, dressed to brave the weather, with his bag in his hand. His landlady was waiting in the hall.

"Are you well-wrapped?" she asked anxiously.

"Och, I'm fine," Tam said.

"A-weel, turn up your collar against the rain's running down your neck," she said, eyeing him with concern. "Och, now! Did I not know it! Bide you here a bit," she said to him.

Tam, although fretting himself to be on his way, waited patiently, and soon she was back with a tartan scarf in her hands. "I said to myself you'd not be wearing a scarf, so I hunted this one out. Are ye daft to be going out on a night like this with your throat bare? Och, it's a mother you're needing, to keep an eye on you, lad."

Tam stood meekly while she wrapped the scarf around his neck and with her own hands adjusted the folds.

"Thank you," he said. "It's good of you."

" 'Tis naught," said she. "Ye need not mind the plaid," she told him. "My husband was a MacDonald, too, so the tartan's your own."

She opened the door, and Tam picked up his bag and stepped out into the storm. "Haste ye back," she said.

The rain had lessened slightly, but it came slantwise on gusts of wind, stinging the face. The sky was filled with scurrying masses of puffy black clouds, and the streaks of green in the west had merged and become one long wide band of pale yellowish green across the distant horizon. As Tam battled his way down the hill, fighting his way against the rain, he heard the bell of the clock in the church tower strike out the hour. He hastened his step. He wanted to reach the station in plenty of time before the guard called the train.

He was hurrying along with his head down, picking

his way along the street as best he could, when he became aware of another wayfarer who seemed to have started up directly before him. The other appeared so suddenly that Tam had to stop dead in his tracks to avoid running into him.

There was a tavern by the way and Tam thought the fellow might have just come from there. But as he looked the stranger in the face someone inside the tavern pushed the curtains of the window aside and light shone out into the street. The man Tam had taken for a stranger was his friend Rab!

"Rab!" exclaimed Tam. "What brings you here?"

"I was looking for you, Tam," said Rab.

"Well, you've found me then," Tam told him. "But had you been a few minutes later you would not have done. I'm away to the station to take the train home, and I must make haste."

"It was in my mind that you would be," said Rab. "I feared you'd be gone, Tam. Do not take the train tonight." Tam pulled his friend into the shelter of a doorway of an empty house beside the tavern, out of the wind and rain.

"Not take the train?" he asked. "Why, I'd be missing a whole day at home if I did not. Why do you not come with me now? We'll both take the train."

"I cannot," Rab said. "I must leave you soon. But hear me, Tam. Go back to your lodgings, now, and bide there until the morrow."

Tam thought it over. Maybe the loss of a day of his holiday would not matter, after all, if he and Rab could be traveling home together the next day.

"Are you listening to me, Tam?" Rab asked impatiently. "Will ye not go back to your rooms and bide there till the morn?"

"Och, well—I will then," Tam said, giving in. He turned to pick up his bag, which he had set down behind him in the entry when they came in. Tam thought he heard Rab give a great sigh of relief, but when he turned back to speak to him again, Rab had slipped off and was gone.

Tam looked up and down the street but there was no sign of Rab at all. He must have gone down the lane by the tavern, Tam thought, as he started up the hill again. The storm was growing wilder and the wind was blowing a terrible gale. Tam found it was all he could do to keep his footing as he climbed the hill. Branches broken from trees, chimney pots and bricks blown down by the wind filled the air and littered the street, and once a great flat piece of something that looked as if it might be the wall of a shed flew, too close for comfort, above his head. Tam was well-accustomed to the wild storms of the Highlands, but in all his life he'd never seen one to compare with this. As he slowly struggled on up the hill there were times that he was all but moving on hands and knees, and he was convinced that only the weight of the bag he carried kept him from flying away on the wind.

Tam was weary, rain-drenched, and chilled to the bone when he reached the house at last and went in. Shutting the door behind him, he seemed to be in a haven after the wild rioting of the storm outside. He leaned against the wall for a minute to get his breath.

The house was dark and silent, with no sight nor sound of life other than himself. The landlady, no doubt, was sitting snugly by the fire in her tidy wee room at the end of the hall, with a nice cup of tea on the stand beside her and one of the pleasant romances she liked to read in her spare time in her hand.

Tam decided that he'd not disturb her to tell her of his return so he went on up the stairs to his rooms. The fire in his sitting room was low but it had not gone out and the room was still warm. Tam put fresh coal upon the fire and stirred it up into a cheerful blaze. Then he got out of his wet clothes and into dry ones. After spreading his rain-soaked garments on the warming rack before the hearth, he mixed himself a good hot toddy to take the chill out of his bones and sat down before the fire himself. It was the first time he had had an opportunity to think about his meeting with Rab. What in the world would be bringing Rab so far from home? And now that he remembered, Rab had not looked himself at all. Thin he was, and very white, and quite unlike the Rab he had left behind him in August, hearty and hale and with the fresh color of a country lad. Had Rab been sick, he wondered? Well, he could ask Rab about it when he saw him on the morrow, but now, what with the hot drink and the heat of the fire, he was too sleepy to think, so he put up the fire guard and went to bed. For a few minutes he lay, warm and drowsy under his blankets, listening to the tumult of the storm without. But, soon, he slept.

When Tam awoke in the morning he could tell as soon as he opened his eyes that the day was already well begun. A pale yellow sunlight came creeping through the windows, as if meekly apologizing for the havoc of the storm during the night. One look at his watch told him that it was past nine o'clock, and he wondered for a moment why his landlady had not brought up his breakfast to him long ago. She was punctual as a rule, arriving on the stroke of half past seven. Surely she would have waked him up, if she had come. Then he remembered that he had not informed her of his return. She would be thinking he was still on his way home, if not already there.

It did not matter, after all. He would dress and go downstairs and ask her to give him a cup of tea and something to go with it for his breakfast. He knew she'd not be minding it at all. He could have gone into the town for his breakfast, of course, but he did not like to leave the house lest Rab should come while he was gone.

As he came down the last steps into the hallway he saw the front door standing open. He heard a babble of voices talking all at once so that a body could not make out a word they said. Above the clatter a woman's voice rose, lamenting like the voice of a Hebridian keen. His landlady stood in the midst of a small group of people, of whom Tam recognized the postman, the milkboy, the constable, Mrs. McNeil the neighbor next door, and half a dozen other persons who lived close by. They were all clustered together upon the steps and at the open door.

Tam stopped on the landing to listen, trying to make out what the folk were so excited about. The first thing he was able to make out was his landlady's saying, "Och, and such a lovely dear lad he was. I'd never find a finer—not if I looked for a year."

"That ye'd not, madam," said the constable. "He always had a cheery smile and a pleasant word when he passed by."

"Aye, so he had," said a neighbor. "He'll be sorely missed, the fine young gentleman."

Tam was intrigued. He wondered what calamity had befallen the unknown young man, and who he was, anyway, to be raising such a ruckus among the folk. He hurried out the front door and onto the top of the front steps to join the group and find out what their clatter was all about.

Tam's landlady, wiping a tear from her cheek, looked up and spied Tam at the top of the steps. He expected her usual smile and greeting, but instead she merely pointed a shaking finger at him and screamed. Every head turned. Postman, milkboy, constable, landlady, and all the neighbors stared in shocked silence at Tam.

"What's amiss?" asked the bewildered Tam.

Then suddenly they were all about him, clutching at him and crying, "You're not dead?" Each of them grabbed at Tam's arms, legs, shoulders, face, to see if he was real.

"Dead?" said Tam. "I am not, then. Why would you be thinking I was dead?"

"Have ye not heard the news, man?" asked the postman.

"News? What news?" asked Tam.

So the constable told him: "The train—the Tay

141 .

Bridge Train! In the great windstorm last night, the middle span blew out, wi' the train just passing over it—and down it tumbled, train and people and all, into the Tay below."

The landlady added, "All those poor folk on the train, drowned dead. And me thinking you were on it, too, it being the train you said you'd be taking." She wiped another tear from her eye, just at the thought.

"And so I would have done," Tam explained. "But I ran into a friend in the town. It was he that persuaded me to wait over until today."

"It was the Lord's mercy, and a miracle, that's what it was," concluded the landlady.

It was the way of life, they said. So many taken, and one spared. They went on about it for a long time.

Needless to say, Tam's spirits were subdued at the thought of such a narrow escape. Only to think—if he'd not met Rab! He'd have gone along to the station, taken the train, and gone into the Tay with the other poor souls who drowned there. And where *was* Rab?

Tam waited all day. Rab did not come. Toward evening he walked down the hill, inquired at hotels and other likely places where Rab might be, but he found no trace of his friend.

The next day, when Rab had still not come, Tam made up his mind that he must have misunderstood his friend. He decided to waste no more of his holiday with waiting, so he set out again on his journey home for Hogmanay. He had a funny feeling that Rab had gone on without him and would be at home when he got there.

Because of the broken bridge, Tam had to go the long way around. Folk were saying it would never be mended. By ferry, by branch line, and by coach, he finally came home on the last day of the year.

Tam's whole family was overjoyed at his arrival. They really had not expected him, since news of the hurricane had already reached them. Knowing of the disaster of the great Tay Bridge, they had felt sure he would not attempt the journey.

After the usual warm family greetings all around, Tam asked them how Rab was. He had looked ill when last Tam had seen him, he told them.

"Aye," said Tam's mother. "The lad had a bad spell o't. He's been long ill, but is mending now. A look at you, Tam, would make him feel all the better, I'm sure."

"So he came home safe, did he?" Tam said. "Och, I owe him my life, that I do! Had it not been that I met up with him on the street on my way to the station, I myself would have been on the Tay Bridge Train, and lost with all the rest. It was Rab that made me hold over till the next day."

"You met Rab?" asked Tam's father sharply. "When was this?"

"When was it?" Tam told him. "When would it be but the night of the great windstorm? December 27th, it was. Och, the wind was rising already when we met. 'Twas all a body could do to keep his footing climbing back up the hill to my lodgings."

"Well, I'll tell you this, Tam," answered his father. "You did not meet Rab that night."

143.

"I did, indeed. I stood for fifteen or twenty minutes and talked with Rab, while he argued that I must go back and wait until the morn. I thought he meant to travel back with me. And then I waited, but he never came."

Said his mother, "Tam, lad, ye couldna have talked to Rab. He's been lying in his bed for the past fortnight."

"He got out of it, then," Tam insisted. "For I myself saw him. Go ask his folk if he was not away."

"I do not need to," said his father. "That night was one I'll not forget. Along about sundown Rab's mother came running to us for help. The lad was bound he'd get up from his bed. Out of his mind with fever, he was, and calling out 'Tam! Tam!' It took me and his father and the cowman to hold him down in his bed, and when he gave up of a sudden, he lay there as white and spent as if he were dead. We did not leave his side until morn, and then we sent for the doctor. But he was only sleeping after all."

Tam was perplexed at this tale. "Well, then, who was it I met then, if not Rab?" he wanted to know.

Tam's grandmother, who had so far not said a word, spoke up tartly. "What would it be but his fetch?"

"Havers!" exclaimed the father. "Auld wives' tales and superstitions!"

The grandmother spoke quietly now, but firmly. "Aye, 'twas the lad's fetch—his living spirit. Rab got the warning that Tam was in danger, and when he could not go himself with the illness on him, and himself held down in his bed, he sent his fetch to hold Tam back from taking the train."

144 .

"I believe you," Tam said. "For if it was not Rab, it must have been as you say. Fetch or spirit, whatever it was, it had Rab's look about it, and it had Rab's voice, and it kept me from taking the Tay Bridge Train."

Tam's father scoffed and blustered, but it was in Tam's mind that he believed in it as much as Tam's grandmother, and Tam's mother and Tam himself did, only he wasn't going to tell them that he did.

As for Rab, all that he remembered was that he had been taken with a terrible fear that some evil hung over Tam's head, and he had fought to go and warn his friend. When they held him down he thought he fell asleep and dreamed that he went and found Tam and put him out of danger. When Rab woke in the morning the fear had left him, and his mind was at rest. He was sure then that Tam was safe.

"I would not know, Tam," said Rab. "But your grandmother could well be right. Maybe my spirit left me and went to warn you, and if so, it must have been my fetch, for, to be sure, it was not my ghost, for I'm not dead."

"Nor I!" Tam said. "Thanks to you."

It was the talk of the countryside for a very long time, and old folk to this day still talk sometimes about the fetch of Rab MacDonald that went to stop his friend Tam on the night of the great windstorm and made him miss the Tay Bridge Train.

The Lass and Her Good Stout
Blackthorn Stick

IN a fishing village on the east coast of Scotland, up above Aberdeen, there dwelt a fishing lad and a bonnie lass that loved each other well. Both of them had been born in the same village and they had been sweethearts ever since they were bairns at school together, and now that they were grown they planned to be married after the herring fishing was over and the catch sold.

But the plans of the two young lovers went awry, for one day when the lad was out in his boat with the fishing fleet a great wind came tearing down upon them from the north, working terrible destruction upon the fishing boats. The storm came up so suddenly and the wind and the waves were so high that there was little the fishermen could do to help themselves. Many a good boat capsized that day to sink into the depths of the sea, and among them was the boat of the fishing lad who loved the bonnie lass. He and his crew were swept off into the sea, and it was only with great difficulty that they were saved by those who had the luck to weather the storm. The fleet limped back to port when the storm was over, but great was the grief in the village, for there were many men who had sailed out at dawn who would never come home again.

They brought the lad home to his mother, half drowned and nearly out of his head with what he'd been through. His mother and his dear lass tended him by turns, and by the end of a fortnight he was on the mend. But if his body was growing stronger his heart was like to break, and how could it be otherwise? A man without a boat of his own would not be earning enough to care for a wife and family. His boat was lost and, without it, he and his lass could not be wed.

"Hush, now," his mother told him. "The Lord will provide. Marry your lass and move in here with your father and me. We'll make do."

But the lad would not put such a burden on his father.

The lass smiled at him fondly. "I'm lucky to have you alive," said she. "Think of the men who lost their lives that day. We must just wait a while longer until we can be wed."

But the lad would take no comfort from what she said.

The lass was a great one for thinking things over, and

she turned their troubles over and over in her mind. One day she came to the lad with a plan. "You sign up with the crew of one of the fishing boats," she told him, "and save what you can. I'll go and find myself a place as a serving lass at one of the crofts, and when I bring my wages back after my time is up, maybe we'll have enough between us to make a start."

He did not care for the notion of her going away but he had no better answer to their problem to offer. So the lass packed her clothes in a bundle and started off to seek work. The lad walked along with her until they came to the highroad, and there he gave her a good stout blackthorn stick that he'd been carrying under his arm.

" 'Tis not much of a gift to be giving a lass," he said. "But it will help you on your way. It's a fine strong stick to lean on, just like yourself."

"Then they parted, and he went back to take his place in the crew of another man's boat, and she went down the highroad that led her away from her home.

She had no luck that first day, for the hiring season was over and the folk at the crofts where she sought a master to hire her were well-suited with the maids they'd got at the hiring fairs. But she went on until she found a shepherd's empty hut at the gloaming, and there she sheltered for the night.

The lass rose with the birds at dawn and broke her fast upon some of the food she had brought along with her in her bundle, and she slaked her thirst in a nearby burn. She washed her face and hands there, too, and tidied her hair, and picking up her bundle and her good stout blackthorn stick she stepped out on her way again, as fresh and bright as the morn itself.

She had no better luck this day than she had had the day before. But she was not disheartened. If she kept on trying she was sure to find a place somewhere, and she had never been one to give up too soon. So the lass went on. Late in the afternoon she came to a very large croft with good fields about it. There were cows to be milked in the barnyard, and hens and geese as well as a big flock of sheep in the brae beyond the fields. The house itself was a big one, much grander than any the lass had ever seen. An extra pair of hands might come in handy in a place the size of that, she thought. So she turned aside from the road and walked up the lane that led to the house.

Now as it happened the farmer at the croft had died that selfsame day. An old man, he'd been, who'd lived his time out and made money hand over hand, through all his years. His oldest son and his wife and all his other sons and daughters lived with him on the croft, so he had never had need of hiring other help. The work was divided among all of them, and it must be admitted that the old man did his share. The croft prospered and they all had what they needed of food and clothing, and were comfortable enough. The trouble was that the old man did all the buying and selling himself, and in all the years of their lives not one of them had ever seen so much as a penny of the old man's gold. They knew he brought money into the house, for droves of sheep and herds of cattle and great loads of farm stuff had been sold through the years, but what he had done with the money paid to him for them not a soul among his family could guess.

It was just a week before that the old man had taken to his bed and told them he'd a mind to die, and in the days since then his sons and daughters had all but torn the house to pieces seeking without success for the gold he had hidden away. When they had seen that morning that he would not last the day, they had filled the final hours of his life trying with all their might to persuade him to tell where he had hidden his hoard. But he only grinned at them and refused to tell them anything at all.

Now there was an old belief among the folk in those parts that if a stranger watched beside a dead person, leaving the door ajar, the dead man would rise from his bed in the middle of the night and answer any question he had been asked while he was lying there. When they saw the lass walking up the lane toward the house, the oldest son said to his wife, "Goodwife, here comes a stranger."

"Aye," said his wife. "A stranger. So it is." Then they looked at each other knowingly, and at the old man's other sons and his daughters.

"Aye—a stranger," they said. "So it is." And without saying more they decided to induce the lass to watch that night beside the dead man.

Now the lass had never heard about this old belief. Folk in her own village knew naught about it or she'd have learned it long before. So she had no notion of what the folk at the croft were planning when she came up the lane to the house and knocked at the door.

"Who's there?" asked the oldest son, as he opened the door.

"A good serving maid seeking a place," answered the lass.

"Och," said the oldest son. "You've come to a house of grief, for our father died this morning, and all of us are worn out with caring for him, for he's been ill for a week." Then the son asked her a few questions, and by her answers he soon knew that she had heard naught of the old belief. So he said, "Well, we're in no need of a serving maid for the croft, but would be willing to hire you to sit and watch by the dead man, so that we may catch a bit of sleep. I'll give you a piece of gold and a piece of silver for the watching tonight."

A piece of gold and a piece of silver was better than nothing, thought the lass, though she had no idea that the dead man's son planned to pay her out of the gold and silver that the dead man had hidden, and which he, the son, could not put his hands on without her. She liked the thought of having a roof over her head, too, even if it did mean sitting up all night with a dead body. So she said she would do it, and they took her into the house. They set her supper before her, and when she had eaten they took her into the front room where the dead man lay. There was a fire burning in the grate and a comfortable chair beside it, facing toward the dead man.

"We'll just be going to bed early," they told the lass, "being that tired out with nursing our poor father here." So they made ready to leave her, but first the oldest son and his wife and the other sons and daughters went over to the dead man, one by one, and whispered something as they bent over him. The lass could not hear the words but she took no interest in what they said.

"Och, the poor things are saying their prayers," she said to herself.

But what they were saying to the dead man was, "Father, where did you lay away your gold?"

Then they all went up the stairs, but the oldest son, before he followed after them, slipped over behind the lass and set the outside door ajar.

The lass set her bundle down beside her, with her good stout blackthorn stick that her lover gave her resting against her knee for company.

The hours went by and she sat on, and now and then she found her head nodding, but she did not fall asleep. When midnight came she got up to mend the fire and that was when she heard a rustle behind her. She looked around and there was the dead man propping himself up on one elbow and giving her a horrible grin.

"Och, now! Lie down there, man, or I'll give you a whack you'll feel!" said she, picking up her stick and shaking it at him. Just then she felt a chilly draft from the half-open door, so she reached around and slammed it shut. When she looked toward the bed again the dead man was lying there, quiet and composed. "Och, it's dreaming I am," said she, and made herself comfortable again beside the fire.

When the folk in the house came downstairs in the morning the oldest son came into the room.

"Did you hear aught in the night?" he asked.

"Nay," said the lass. "All was quiet. Except for once when I felt a draft and pushed the door shut, so that it slammed. If it was that noise you were hearing, I made it myself."

"Och, well, I see," said the oldest son. "Will you watch again tonight? 'Twill be the last, since the burial is tomorrow. We'll pay you the same as before."

"I'll not be minding," answered the lass. "I'll watch again." So she had breakfast and slept the whole day through until evening, when they woke her up.

She had her supper, and then she went back to the room where the dead man lay and made herself comfortable by the fire again, sitting with her good stout blackthorn stick that her lover gave her in her hand.

The oldest son and his wife and the other sons and daughters passed by the bed, one by one, and whispered to the dead man as they had the night before. "Father, where did you hide your money?" they whispered, but the lass heard not a word, nor did she try to hear.

Then they all went upstairs, the oldest son last of all, but this time when he set the door ajar he stuck a block of wood in the hinge so that the door could not be shut.

The lass sat by the fire and the hours seemed longer than they had the night before, but she took comfort from the thought that she would not have to watch another night. Then midnight came, and she heard the stirring of the covers on the bed. She looked, and there was the dead man, propped up on one elbow and giving her a horrible grin. The lass took her good stout blackthorn stick that her lover gave her in her hand

154 .

and cried out, "Lie down there decently, man, or I'll give it to you good."

Then she felt the cold draft from the open door and shaking her stick at the dead man, she pushed at the door to shut it, but that she could not do, for the block that the man's son had put in the hinge would not let it shut.

"The de'il take this door!" the lass cried in vexation. "Why will it not shut, the way it should!"

She turned back to the fire to warm herself, for a cold wind was blowing upon her, and then she saw the dead man leaping out of his bed and making for the open door. The lass caught up her good stout blackthorn stick that her lover gave her and off she went after the dead man. As he went out through the doorway she gave him a swinging blow with the stick on his backside and cried out, "Come away, man! Come back to your bed and lay yourself down like a decent body. 'Tis not seemly for you to go on this way, it is not indeed!"

But the dead man reached around him and caught the stick by its end and held it fast. She would not let go and he would not let go, so off they went together, both holding on to the stick for dear life, off and away over the countryside. Down the road they went for a mile or so, and then he turned aside and at top speed legged it over the moor. He led her a merry chase up hill and down dale, through heather and broom and bracken, through copse and underbrush, where the twigs of the bushes reached out like clutching hands to catch her by the hair and hold her back. The low branches of the trees slapped cruelly at her face as she and the dead man rushed by. The moon looked down and laughed to see the sport, and their shadows danced merrily before them in the moonlight as the two of them sped along. But she had no mind to lose her good stout blackthorn stick that her lover gave her, so she held fast and on they went until the dawn began to show signs of breaking. Then, in a trice, the dead man turned himself about and raced back the way he had come. Suddenly, they were at the house once again. They came through the door into the room, just as the cock in the rafters of the barn began to crow out the morn. Then the dead man let go of his end of the stick and going over to the bed lay down.

He fixed his staring eyes on the lass and finally said, "In the chimney under the thatch it is, and you'd not have known it, had you ever let go of the stick." Then he shut his eyes and crossed his arms upon his breast and to look at him lying there so calm and peaceful, one would never have known he'd been out of his bed that night.

The lass, once she had got her breath again, tidied her hair and set her skirts to rights. She went to the door and found the block of wood stuck in the hinge. She took the block out and shut the door of the house and sat down in her chair by the fire, with her good stout blackthorn stick that her lover gave her at her knee, and waited for the folk in the house to wake up and come downstairs again.

The goodwife was the first one down, and when she saw the dead man lying quiet in his bed and the lass no less quiet in her chair, she began to weep and wail.

"Och," she cried loudly. "The auld man's secret will go with him into his grave if he did not tell it to you last night, for we'll not have another chance to find out where his money is hidden since he'll be buried today."

The lass turned her eyes from the fire and looked at the goodwife. She was a clever lass and could see how they had made use of her, without telling her what they were about. "Now hold your tongue!" she told the wife of the oldest son. "I've had the de'il of a time this night, all because of your auld man, but in the end he told his secret to me."

Then she told the goodwife all that had happened between her and the dead man, but when she came to the part of her story about what the dead man had said to her, she held back and did not seem to want to tell.

"Och!" cried the oldest son's wife. "What an awkward piece you are! Tell me, lass, what did he say?"

"Och, well," said the lass. "Somehow it goes against me to be repeating what he told me. After all, 'tis sure he wasn't wanting you to know or he'd have told you himself. No doubt you asked him about it while he was dying, the poor old creature."

The sons and the daughters were all awake by now. With all the commotion in the house who could sleep? They all crowded into the room where the dead man lay and there was the goodwife cursing and coaxing the lass by turns. When they found out what the trouble was, they added their voices to hers, and such a to-do you never heard.

But the lass sat quietly in her chair all the while, as

if she had not heard a word. All the answer they got from her did them little good.

"I'm thinking it over," was all she'd say.

Then the oldest son of the family, himself having a bit more sense than the rest of them, shushed them all up and gathered them all into a far corner of the room where they whispered together for a while. Then the oldest son left them and came over to the lass and stood before her.

"Look ye now," he said quietly to the lass. "My father loved his money more than anything or anyone else in the world when he was living. If he wanted to hide it from us then, we let him have his way, to be sure. But now that he's dead his gold is of no use to him for they'll not be letting him fetch it along with him where he's gone. All of us worked as hard as he did to help him pile it up. Should we not have the good of it now that he's dead and does not need it any more?"

But the lass only listened and said nothing.

"Come, now," said the oldest son in a wheedling way. "You'll never be the worse off for telling us what the old man said. You shall have ten pieces of gold for every hundred the old man had, if you can tell us where he hid it away."

"I'll have to think it over," said the lass.

So they waited and waited while the lass was thinking it over, and a very long time went by. Then the lass said, "Write on a piece of paper what you have promised me, and give me the paper to hold. Happen I'll tell you what the poor old man said to me."

So they wrote down on a piece of paper that the lass

was to get ten pieces of gold for every hundred that the old man had laid away, and signed it with all their names. They gave it to the lass, and when she had put it safely in her pocket, she told them what they wanted to know.

"It's in the chimney under the thatch," said she. "That's what the dead man said."

Then they climbed up to the rafters, and hidden under the thatch they found a cupboard craftily built into the stones of the chimney. They opened the cupboard and on the shelves were bags and bags of gold that the old man had been hiding there for fifty years or more. They took it down and counted it out on the table, and out of every hundred pieces the lass got her ten. Since she had their promise in writing they could not very well give her less, nor would they have done so, being that thankful to her for finding out where it had been hidden. It made a good sum when it was all handed over to her, and after she'd counted it for herself to make sure she'd had her rights, she asked them for a bag to carry it home in, which they gave her willingly.

Then she went off back down the road toward home with the bag of gold in one hand and her good stout blackthorn stick that her lover gave her in the other. She kept on going, one foot after the other, until she came to the fishing village where she was born.

Sitting there on the jetty, looking out to the sea, was the lad she loved. He was mourning two losses, for not only was his bonnie fishing boat gone forever but his dear lass whom he loved so well had left him, too. The mood in his heart was so dark that he doubted that he'd ever lay eyes on her again. With his back to her and himself so deep in thought he did not see her coming toward him, nor know she was near, until she sat down beside him and plumped the bag of gold in his lap.

"There, lad," said the lass. "There's our fortune, and you shall buy a grand new boat, bigger and better in every way than the one that went down in the sea. And there will be enough to build us a house to live in when we are married."

But it was not the sack of gold he was minding. He let it slip from his knee unheeded and reached out to take his lass in his arms. "I could do without a ship and a house," he told her. "But I could never see my way to doing without your dear self."

The fishing boat was bought and it was bigger and better than any one in the harbor. The house was built, too, and not one in the village was finer. The lad and the lass were married and settled down happily together. And as years passed by many and many a time she told her children and her grandchildren also, the story of her adventure with the dead man and the good stout blackthorn stick.

Glossary

an dun na cuantaiche: (an dûn na kŭăn′-ttech-à), the castle of the rover.

an traigh bhean: (an træ̂-y vvhen), the woman's shore.

aye: always, forever.

bens: hills, mountains.

Ben Nevis: a mountain in the Highlands near Loch Linne; at 4,406 feet, it is the highest point in the British Isles.

bothan: (baw′-hawn), a hut.

braw: brave, hearty, brawny.

cailleach: (kăly′-ak), an old woman.

caillean: (kai-lean′), a young girl, colleen.

cairn: a quarry, a pile of stones.

callant: a flashy young fellow, a gallant.

catteran: a Highland freebooter.

ceilidh: (kay′-lee), a gathering, a party, a merrymaking, a visit.

clachan: a small hamlet.

cleev: skein, as of wool.

coof: a fool.

coronach: a ritualistic death chant or song.

de'il: not a; a colloquial expression, contraction of "Devil."

dule: grief.

fash: worry, bother.

fipple flute: a kind of small wind instrument.

ghillie: a manservant.

greeting: weeping.

grue: curdle.

havers! nonsense!

hiero! an exclamation like "So!" or "Well now!"

Hogmanay: New Year in Scotland.

howk: to throw oneself into a task.

lawks! a mild expression of surprise; a corruption of "Lord!"

liefer: rather.

losh: an exclamation combining "Lord!" and "Gosh!"

mo chu: (mo cū), my dog.

mo graidh: (mo grah/-ēē), my dear.

nighean mhúirninn: (nyè/-un mûér-nin), beloved girl.

och! ochone! oh! o-o-o-oh!

omadhaun: (ō/-maw-hawn), a crazy fellow, a fool.

Sassenach: Saxon, particularly an Englishman.

sgian-dubh: (skēān/-dŭgh), dirk, dagger.

shielan: group of shielings.

shieling: (shēē/-ling), a cottage.

shoon: shoes.

sluagh: (sloo/-ah), a great many.

thole: bear, abide, withstand.

toom: empty.

Sorche Nic Leodhas:
A Remembrance

Sorche Nic Leodhas (Sor-a Nic Ly-os) is a Gaelic name. In English, it means "Claire, daughter of Louis." Louis Gowans' daughter was christened LeClaire Louise, in Youngstown, Ohio, in 1897. In 1900 the Gowans family settled in Pittsburgh, Pennsylvania, after several moves back and forth between Chicago and New York. There, LeClaire married her first husband, Amos Risser Hoffman, when she was nineteen. Two years later, in 1918, she was left a young widow with one son. Her husband had been stricken in the influenza epidemic of that year. She moved to New York, attending classes at Columbia University for a while. Several years later she met her second husband. As LeClaire Gowans Alger, she returned to Pittsburgh, where she was to live the remainder of her years.

In 1960, with the publication of her first book of Scottish tales, Mrs. Alger adopted the pseudonym, Sorche Nic Leodhas. She had two reasons for writing under a name other than her own. The Gaelic name, of course, lent an air of authenticity to the work she had begun with *Heather and Broom*. But there was a deeper reason for the author's use of a pen name. The Sorche Nic Leodhas afforded her a cloak of anonymity and provided her an escape from the publicity she had always feared. Basically shy and introspective, the author shunned the limelight in every respect, seldom allowing details of her private life to be published, even in the pages of her many books.

When her picture book *Always Room for One More* won the Caldecott Medal in 1966, Mrs. Alger wrote her true feelings to one of her dear friends, Virginia Chase, a librarian. She said, "I am glad for Nonnie [Hogrogian, the illustrator], who deserves the honor; glad for Holt [the publisher], who collectively reap the kudos from it; and sorry for myself if the award attracts undesired attention to me. . . . You see, to me, it is not a question of false modesty—nor has it been a matter of sour grapes because my books haven't won awards in the past. I have never wanted awards because the fanfare that follows seems to me to be an invasion of privacy. There are a few people so firmly fixed in my affection that I never feel that I need a shell to crawl into. But the public unveiling of personal life too aptly known as 'publicity' gives me the 'orrors!"

This horror of publicity no doubt had its roots in the author's childhood. She had always been carefully protected from contact with strangers by her parents. Considered a frail and sensitive child, her own father tutored her at home from the time she was three years old and could first read and write. She never attended more than a single full day of public school. Yet her education was thorough and disciplined. Her father took her through *Julius Caesar* from beginning to end, with no shirking or skipping allowed of the difficult Latin. She grew to admire the logic and magnitude of the great man's mind. Caesar remained her second hero all her life. Her father was her first.

At his knee, LeClaire learned history and geography so well that she could draw physical and historical maps of many countries. She learned, too, to read and write German, Italian, Spanish, and French through his patient instruction. During the day, while her father worked, LeClaire would take her books and accompany the family doctor on his rounds. While he visited his patients, the young girl would wait in his buggy, studying her lessons for the evening review with her father. It was a solitary life, and very scholarly for such a young child, but never dull to one who had inherited the excitement of learning from her parent.

So successful was Mr. Gowans' teaching that when his daughter made up her mind to go to college, she was able to enter Columbia University without difficulty. Back in Pittsburgh, she took entrance examinations at Duquesne University and was placed in the senior class.

Yet this precosity and personal discipline had its effect on the child grown adult. She had become much too shy to attend the usual functions when her book *Thistle and Thyme* was named runner-up for the Newbery Medal. She permitted no one outside her immediate family to visit her at home. Even her phone was unlisted, and finally removed. And any request from the publishers to offer something of her personal history to the jackets of her books met with a consistent "No."

Only among children was Mrs. Alger able to easily converse, telling them stories and talking to them about their own interests and encounters. She had attended library school at the University of Pittsburgh, and although she had never received a formal degree, she worked as an "itinerant librarian" for over thirty-five years. One day of her week was devoted to the central branch of Pittsburgh's Carnegie Library. She had the "Story Hour" there for many years. Five other days were meted out to branch libraries at public and parochial schools, mostly in the city's underprivileged areas. She had no fear of walking the streets on dark winter evenings as she left work for the long streetcar rides home. She knew all of the children in the neighborhoods, and therefore most of their parents, as well.

It was during these car rides to and from her posts that she did much of her writing. Before the publication of the first collection of Scottish tales, Mrs. Alger had written three other books for children, under her own name. They were published in the 1950's by Harper's. *The Golden Summer* and *Jan and the Wonderful Mouth Organ* both centered about children growing up in Czechoslovakia. She had drawn her material from the families she knew in one of Pittsburgh's Slavic neighborhoods.

Dougal's Wish was the story of a Scotch-American family, and took place in the farmlands of Pennsylvania. The background tapped here was Mrs. Alger's

170 .

own Gaelic lineage. Her mother was Clan Stewart, her father Clan Cameron—both Highland Scotch. As a child, LeClaire had been filled with tales from Scotland, circulated at family get-togethers by her own parents, grandparents, and droves of other, more distant relatives, many of whom, like her grandparents, had been born in that mysterious and romantic land. She had always dreamed of going there, to see the land and hear its tales from its own people for herself. She said she'd never get lost there; of all countries she knew Scotland best and never tired of describing it to the generations that came after her. Like a blind person who knows a face by feeling it, Sorche Nic Leodhas knew her Scotland by reading its history, its maps, and its legends. The fingers of her mind knew the land well, if her eyes themselves had never seen it.

With *Dougal's Wish* the seeds were sown for an idea that had long been taking shape in its author's mind. The seeds took nourishment from a long family tradition of storytelling and grew into the thirteen books of Scottish lore by Sorche Nic Leodhas.

But Sorche Nic Leodhas did not live to make her journey to the homeland. Nor did she live to complete this book, *Twelve Great Black Cats*. But it has been completed nevertheless. Before she became ill in the fall of 1969, she had been working on this collection of eerie tales. She had eight of ten stories written, but had not been able to decide on the last two. She had three in mind, but only wanted two to complete the volume. She was concerned that the mood at the end be just right.

To solve her dilemma, she consulted a second person. As her great-niece, I had grown up listening to her stories. And as I got older, I began to work for my aunt as well. As her own ability to handle the load of typing and filing and correspondence lessened with age, I took on more and more of these tasks. And she had asked me to double-check time-signatures and technical details of *A Scottish Song Book* she had done in 1968. But she had never actually consulted me about material for a manuscript. Now she had asked me to choose the last two stories for her book.

Over dinners on Friday nights, my aunt would tell me her stories, just as though I were a little girl again, and she were merely entertaining me. Once we had talked all three over and made the difficult decision, she set to work on notes for the two stories we had chosen. But before she had finished this preliminary task, she fell ill.

After her death, I began to collect what notes she had made in order to write the two stories myself. I found that the work she had done consisted of catch phrases taken directly from the stories as she had told them to me. Mentally she had them completed before she ever began to work on paper, so these words and phrases were simply clues for me to follow in re-assembling her two, fully fleshed stories. My years of experience in working for my aunt, the notes she herself left, and a fairly clear recollection of just how it was that she had told me the tales stood me in good stead. The result is, I believe, two stories by Sorche Nic Leodhas, merely retold by someone else.

A Remembrance

In preparing this book for publication it occurred to a great many people that it is time, at last, to give something of the author's life to her readers. During her lifetime, all of her family and her many close friends regarded her as an intelligent and remarkably gifted woman. As such, and as friends and loved ones, we respected without exception her wish for privacy. It was the necessity of appearing in public and responding to any curiosity that gave the author her strong aversion to publicity of any kind. This tribute to her life and work, in the form of her own book and these brief words about her, surely could not trouble Sorche Nic Leodhas now.

Jenifer Jill Digby
August 28, 1970

About the Artist

VERA BOCK was born in St. Petersburg, Russia, and came to the United States with her family while still a child. Miss Bock returned to Europe to study drawing and painting and went to England for extensive study of wood engraving, illuminating, and heraldry. Many of the books Miss Bock has illustrated and designed have appeared in the American Institute of Graphic Arts Children's Book shows and Fifty Books exhibits.

Sorche Nic Leodhas greatly admired Vera Bock's artistry in her illustrations for *By Loch and by Lin* and *Sea-Spell and Moor-Magic*. Miss Bock has used wash drawings—accented with charcoal, pencil, paint, and chalk—for *Twelve Great Black Cats,* giving them her special, eerie quality.

The display type is set in Bodoni Book and the text type in Caledonia. The book is printed by offset.

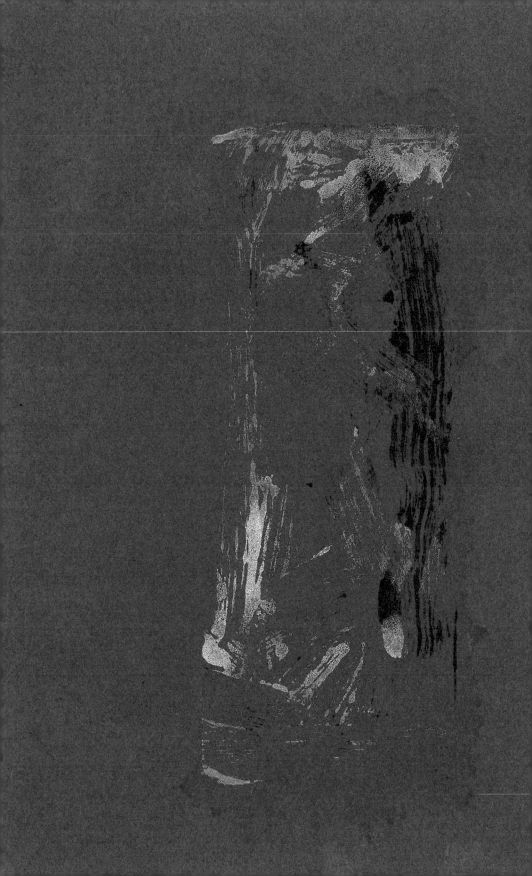